HALF-THREE IN GALWAY

To Joan,

May you be blessed with the strength of heaven ... the light of the sun and the radiance of the moon ... the splendor of fire ... the speed of lightning ... the swiftness of wind ... the depth of the sea ... the stability of earth and the firmness of rock.

from the breastplate of St. Patrick

Suzanne Riley

HALF-THREE IN GALWAY

Suzanne Riley

www.1stbooks.com

ISBN: 0-75966-268-1

This book is printed on acid free paper.

1stBooks - rev. 11/20/01

Contents

For
Matthew and Sarah,
Watching you in love is like a fresh breath of life.

Foreword and Acknowledgements

When finally I persuaded my husband Richard to go to Ireland to visit our son Matthew, who was attending Queens University in Belfast, Northern Ireland, I had yet to come clean with my intention to haul a laptop computer along. Email and web surfing was then quite new to me, and I couldn't fathom being out of touch with friends and family for a whole month. I had latched onto the online chat routine with fervor, testing Richard's patience when I tied up the lines for hours on Saturday mornings.

On to Ireland we journeyed, with great anticipation, for this wouldn't be simply a tour of the country - we were there to help Matt make arrangements for his upcoming wedding to Sarah Rogers, who would be joining us two weeks later. Matt, a student of his Irish heritage, had insisted since age twelve that *if* he ever got married, he'd do the deed in Ireland. We had always thought this a charming, if droll, declaration, but we hadn't thought he meant *Northern* Ireland. However, our anxious concerns about the barely subdued unrest there were dispelled the moment we landed and experienced the gracious gentility of the Ulster people.

The wedding, which took place in County Cavan (just south of the Ulster border) on an abnormally cold December day in an unheated church — excuse me, I must interject here that it wasn't that the church was typically unheated during Mass...it was warmed by the congregation's collective body heat, and had we known this, we'd have invited the entire village of Belturbet — the holy water well was frozen over, for pity's sake! Anyway, the wedding turned out to be the most romantic wedding ever. Sarah was radiantly beautiful in her white flowing gown and green hooded cloak. Our tall, handsome Matt looked dashing in his tuxedo. Two farm girls played "Danny Boy" and "Killyshandra Girl", and Anthony, the corner store proprietor, photographed the event with his ancient camera. My knees were knocking from the cold, but our hearts were warmed watching these two young adults so in love.

Anyway, my trusty laptop accompanied us indeed, and from my journals, a year later the story *Half-Three in Galway* began to take form. At the time, I was working long hours in a job that demanded much time and energy, and the story of Maggie and Thomas was often necessarily shelved, though never forgotten. Thus it was four years in writing. But here it is, and I have the following people to thank for their help and support.

Thanks to my sister Dianne Heaney, to my friend Joan Bouchard, and to a superb editor, Liz Morrill, for reading and offering their thoughtful, constructive critique.

Loving thanks to my dear friend Susan Rand, for her encouragement and her tireless hours editing the book with me, but especially for the laughs we shared in the process. Everyone with whom I share Susan's friendship will understand well my belief that every person should be blessed with a friend like her.

David Trufant, who made online chat such a stitch and encouraged me in the early stages of this book, conceptualized several pieces of the plot with me and kept reminding me to forebear and persist.

Allen Gerber responded instantly with kudos and helpful advice when I told him, "I've written a novel," and he continually shows genuine faith in my ability to write, no matter what the purpose. For this I give him many thanks.

Lastly, I owe everlasting gratitude to Richard for many things, but mostly for putting up with me and my ways, and who would likely say to this, "We're partners...just doing my job."

Prologue

Three men bringing up the rear of the funeral procession trudged along unevenly, one of them anxiously scanning the landscape. The mournful drone of the wind across the top of the hill seemed to warn them of yet more troubles to come. "Go away, go now," it moaned with monotonous repetition. For a moment the two Irishmen and the American thought the woman heard it, too. She turned and exchanged worried glances with them over the bowed heads of the funeral-goers before turning and gently clasping the arm of the grief-stricken woman beside her.

"You don't think they'd come up here, do you?" asked the American.

The older Irishman stumbled over a rut on the path and steadied himself. "Aye," he murmured, "no question about it. They may be right here in the crowd for all we know, posing as old cronies from the city." He stopped abruptly and looked sharply at the other two.

"It's worth it, you know," he said. "We have to do this...agreed?"

"Aye," answered the young man from Ulster eagerly.

"Yes," the American said in grim but firm agreement. "There's a legacy and a future to be protected."

The group of villagers, friends, and relatives who had reached the gravesite formed a circle behind the priest and the widow, surrounding the casket. The burial place had been carefully chosen, not for the deceased, because everyone assumed his spirit had long since left and gone on to a higher world. For those remaining behind, a small bench under a nearby tree provided a place for respite and reflection; beyond the cemetery, spread below the hill was a comforting vision of woods and lake.

The drone of the wind faltered, then switched suddenly into a screeching whine, like the howl of a banshee, for a few moments before it died back. A small child began to cry, and the American shivered.

But then a sunray sheared through an opening in the colorless skies and aimed its brightness on a wide patch of ground across the hill that encircled the crowd of black-clad mourners. The three men stared at the calming light and then at each other. The sad old Irishman nodded to the casket. Indeed, it was a sign, telling them to proceed with their plan.

---

chapter 1

THOMAS

Who, of men, can tell
That flowers would bloom, or that green fruit
*   would swell*
To melting pulp, that fish would have bright mail,
The earth its dower of river, wood, and vale,
The meadows runnels, runnels pebble-stones,
The seed its harvest, or the lute its tones,
Tones ravishment, or ravishment its sweet
If human souls did never kiss and greet?

John Keats, 1795-1821 (London)

January 1996

The huge jet began its final descent through clear, crisp skies over the Manhattan cityscape. Violet skies, Thomas noted as he gazed out the window and stretched his legs, stiff from the six-hour flight. Then he frowned as the color filled his thoughts with recognition. *Violet...deep blue violet...extraordinary violet...there's only one other place I've seen that incredible color. Maggie.*

"Oh yes, it's an enchanting place," said a lady with a soft brogue sitting directly behind Thomas, "and it isn't likely you'll soon find another like it. You'll think you've been swept back fifty years. I'm from Dublin myself, and things are more modern there, but out in the countryside..."

"I've heard that," replied the woman next to her. "Now that I've seen Scotland, I'd like to visit Ireland next time over."

"Quite different from Scotland, and Wales and England, too. It's there, across the sea from the UK, its own island, green as green can be, with a soft air that caresses you."

And, thought Thomas as he listened to the Irish woman describing her beloved home, *there's a quietness about it that soothes the over-exercised soul, and a quaintness that banishes troubles from a weary mind. Just what I need right now.*

The woman continued in a dreamy, unhurried voice, sipping her bitter airplane coffee between phrases, talking as though she sorely missed the land she left only hours ago: "Thatched roof cottages, sheep grazing in emerald pastures framed by stone walls, remains of castles and monasteries, walks along boreens canopied by ancient trees, timeless music played on the pennywhistle pouring out the windows of intimate pubs, peat burning in broad stone fireplaces to warm you even on the most chilling winter day. Ah, 'tis a lovely place, my Eire."

"My goodness," said the other woman, "you sound like a poet."

The Irish woman chuckled. "We all do, dear...it's ingrained in the Irish soul. Everyone writes or sings or acts. We're a wistful lot."

Thomas closed his tired eyes, the fatigue stinging

behind his lids. He willed his mind away from the present and summoned up the colorful descriptions in the travel literature hc had read on his long flight over from the U.S. a few weeks ago. *"Eire...a land embedded in ageless beauty...people of a mischievous, gentle nature...politics fraught with a history of angst and bloody, bitter dissent...culture brimming with music, dance, art, religion, and a spoken tradition in heartfelt words and folk tales and songs...a place that must surely have been created for kindling the embers within a romantic heart. There are sparks of newness, of excitement, of wonder, there amidst the crumbling ruins. Ever changing, forever the same."*

As the aircraft banked hard to circle for landing, the maze of buildings, waterways and roadways filled the window. He scanned for familiar sights...the Chrysler Building, the Statue of Liberty, the Empire State Building, Staten Island, a glimpse of Central Park. Buildings, industry, everyday twentieth century life. No rolling pastures, no ancient stone walls, no monastic ruins...back home in the now and present.

He sat up straighter. Hopefully, the package had been delivered to his co-op by now. For the hundredth time since he'd boarded the plane, he thought through the steps he must take to carry out his part of the plan. Mentally he checked them off: get the package, contact the others, secure technical experts, set up financing, arrange the production process.

He frowned and shifted away from the window, his thoughts turning inward again, recounting once more the unexpected succession of events that led him to this time and place. His mind captured and hung onto an odd, Picasso-like image of legs and buttons and film and bright blue-violet eyes teasing, crying, sparkling with laughter and tears. He swallowed, a reaction to the unexplainable sensa-tion of chocolate with a hint of orange flavor washing across his taste buds. Thomas blinked when the images melded together and transformed into a clear vision of Maggie's face. He turned to look out the window again. Then he closed his eyes, the loneliness permeating his body and mind, pressing on his heart with a heaviness that showed in his face.

Mechanically he shuffled off the plane behind the Irish woman and her flight companion. Following a long row of passengers through baggage handling and customs, he boarded the shuttle bus headed for the long-term parking lot. A whole other world it was, he thought, as the shuttle ride recalled for him a cheerier journey on a bus down a narrow, paved lane lined with ancient low stone walls and fringed with deep green grasses and moss. This ride across the gray colored tarmac and cold concrete was tainted with hydrocarbon exhaust pollution and city noises. The tight oppressiveness of the city hit him full-fisted in his face, and he longed for the clear, pure air of where he'd just been.

"Visiting, or coming home?" The shuttle driver's ques-tion interrupted his thoughts, and he was glad for it.

"Coming home."

"Long trip?"

"Yeah, how'd you know?"

"Not too many fellas carry luggage that has to be checked unless they have to."

"How's the weather been?"

"Okay, a little colder than normal, but you're back at a good time...they say a warm spell's heading this way...maybe even melt some of that ice."

"Ah, good." Not much more to say, and the driver con-centrated as he entered heavy traffic.

Thomas allowed his musing to float back to the Connemara Mountains, the ocean bluffs, the thatched roof cottages dotting the countryside of County Galway. As if he were riding on the wings of a seagull, Thomas imagined himself gliding along the rocky coastline, dipping inland over the golden wheat-colored wild grasses of the hills, spotting a herd of wild ponies, flying, sailing, feeling the whoosh and slap of the cold winter wind that whipped his hair and caught his breath, filling his lungs with salty air that stung until tears moistened the corners of his eyes.

The smack of the bus door startled him back to this place, the city, the parking lot.

"This your Jag, sir?" the driver leaned over to get a better look at the sleek car next to where he had stopped the van, obviously admiring it.

"Yep, it sure is...that's Eva," he said with a proud smile.

They had pulled into the fenced corral with high security and bright lights that distinguished the section where high-priced luxury and sport cars were parked, all of them no doubt left there by CEO's and executives with handsome salaries and little time to enjoy their expensive toys. Not him. Neither rich nor workaholic, Thomas had splurged the day he noticed the sleek black 1978 Jaguar at the Barrett-Jackson classic car auction and pulled the "For Sale" sign out of the window after shaking hands with the owner. This car, like a well-tended thoroughbred racehorse, demanded to be exercised, preened, and pampered.

"Eva, huh?"

"Yeah, somehow the name just seemed to suit her."

As men will do, the driver smiled knowingly and nodded, even though he had no idea why a black Jaguar should be called Eva. Thomas stood and began to collect his bags, but the driver stopped him. "Here, sir, let me get your bags for you."

"Thanks."

He swiped the wetness from his eyes and opened the trunk of the Jaguar, covered now with the dwindling vestiges of winter snow, melting under the sun's rays despite the freezing temperature. The sharp brightness of the sun on the windshield blinded him for a moment, and Thomas longed for the soft Irish climate, the light, smooth, misty feeling of oneness between body and atmosphere. He thanked the driver again and tipped him generously.

A sigh, a frown, and gritting his teeth, Thomas pulled his keys out of his pocket, climbed into his Jag and caressed its old, familiar seat. The folds and tufts of the soft tan leather upholstery were velvet to his touch. He ran his hand across the dash and brushed away specks of dust, then pulled out his handkerchief and wiped a smudge on the rearview mirror. *Yeah, okay,* he thought with a smile, *I can handle this...it's good to be home.* He turned the key, growled out loud in unison with the roar of the ignition, and laughed with the boyish delight his Jag evoked every time he climbed behind the wheel.

Turning into the brisk, multi-laned traffic out of LaGuardia, he was reminded again how far he was from the quiet, laid-back Irish countryside and its meandering, narrow lanes. He squeezed the wheel and braced himself for the change of pace. The engine responded immediately as he accelerated and moved into the far left lane heading for Queensboro Bridge, which would take him home to East Fiftieth Street in Manhattan.

* * * * * *

As the elevator door opened on his floor, a tense frown crossed his face and his brow furled with concern as he remembered to expect the package. Opening the door to his co-op, he immediately looked down. There on the floor in front of him rested a white Federal Express envelope. He tore it open and removed a flat manila envelope labeled with one word written in small, squarish, handwritten letters: "Keats." Thomas inspected the sealed flap, ran his finger along the edge, and stopped when he found a frayed edge, barely visible, and a strip where the glue had smeared. He touched the clasp, noting its irregularities that indicated it had been bent back and forth more than once. He examined it more closely, then slit the edge of the flap and pulled the contents half out of the envelope. He shuffled through the pages, assuring himself that the material inside was as it should be, and set the envelope on the desk next to his computer. Sighing, he realized that he could relax for the first time in days...finally he could finish this project and get back to a normal life. Finally? Now it seemed his only choice.

He threw his luggage onto the bed, flung his black topcoat carelessly on top of his bags, and picked up the phone to check his voice-mail. Changing his mind, he hung up and pulled off his wool sweater, hiking boots, and jeans, leaving them in a jumbled pile on the floor. A good, hot shower, he thought, that's what I need first. A few minutes later he stepped out of the steaming bathroom, climbed into faded, hole-ridden sweats, and padded around the apartment as if re-acquainting himself with an old, comfortable friend. He filled the teapot and turned the burner on high.

Back in the bedroom, he picked up the phone once more. Another idea struck him, and again he hung up the phone. He set up his laptop at his desk and switched it on.

Quickly he paced through the steps to re-subscribe to the online service he'd cancelled only a few days ago. When prompted for a screen name, impulsively he entered the name *Cavanbound* and added a password. *That's a tad reckless of you, wouldn't you say?* he admonished himself. But he ignored the thought and headed directly to a chat area. Seconds later, the screen locked and he was dumped offline.

"Lost carrier," the screen read.

"Shit," Thomas said to his computer.

He walked into the kitchen to make a cup of tea. Recalling Maggie's instructions ("There's only one way to prepare tea correctly, Thomas," she'd insisted), he heated the water to boiling and placed the teabag in the mug. There was no honey in the cupboard, so a dried up packet of artificial sugar would have to do. He poured the boiling water into the cup too fast, though, and the diet sugar bubbled the water over the cup onto the counter. Damn, he'd have to practice more to get Maggie's instructions down pat and not use substitutes. He wiped the slosh from the counter with a paper towel and twisted the bottom of the mug on the towel to dry it off, tossing the crumpled rag in the sink.

Neatness wasn't a high priority for Thomas, but he suddenly recognized with a wry smile the influence she'd had on him that way, too. He reached for the towel, aimed for the garbage can, then defiantly threw it back to the sink, where it narrowly missed and fell to the floor. *There now, Maggie ol' girl,* he thought, *how d'ya like them apples?* Mug in hand, he returned to his computer to try again.

This time he logged on easily and found mail waiting for him, signaling with a perky beep. *Mail already?* he wondered and then recalled the usual welcome letter from the service. He headed again for the chat rooms, contemplating which room to try and opting for the familiar Over

Forty group he had visited occasionally the past year. He watched the dialogue scroll up his screen, found some old acquaintances chattering away, and almost responded to them. Then he remembered, *I've got a new name, they won't know me.* Another hesitation, and he exited the room and double-clicked on another one named "IrishPub2". The scrolling dialogue moved fast, to his liking, so he typed, "Howdy from a Yank...are the natives restless?"

Immediately several people responded. "Welcome, boyo," "How's tricks across the ocean?" "What time is it over there...we're pouring Guinness, would you like a draw, lad?" One particular response caught his attention. He stared at the name on the screen — GalwayDrm. It stirred recent memories, forcing a rueful smile from Thomas, and he shook his head roughly as if to dispatch his thoughts into thin air. Yet he looked again as GalwayDrm wrote, "Hey there, Cavanbound, care for a spot of tea?"

"Thanks," he answered, tapping the keys as fast as his tired fingers would allow, "but I've got some. Now if you want a good cup of tea, allow me."

GalwayDrm retorted with letters that formed words on the screen in quick succession: "Go for it, honey, I expect you know how to boil water."

Something in the response glimmered familiarly to him. *Ah nuts, you're just missing Ireland and her*, he admonished himself. Yet he paid closer attention to the conversation. He tapped out a reply to GalwayDrm, "And when it boils over, I'm pretty quick with a towel, too...LOL."

chapter 2

CHANCE ENCOUNTER - MAGGIE

Manhattan, weeks earlier

The twenty-eighth floor office was small, barely accommodating a desk, file cabinet and bookshelf. Neat...in fact, painstakingly organized except for the jumbled stacks of folders and papers Thomas had carelessly tossed on his desk...the bookshelf held a row of three-ring notebooks identically labeled with the Holmes Company logo...production projections, schedules, product development plans, annual reports, sales manuals. The wastebasket had been emptied, the paper clip holder was filled, and the dry erase project board was not only erased but also washed clean.

It wasn't Thomas's doing. His new assistant Matt followed him around like a worshipful Beagle and had taken on the monumental task of organizing Thomas's office. No one would recognize Thomas's nature in the pristine shelves and thriving plants with shiny green leaves. He scorned neatness and tolerated it only because he liked Matt. Taped to the side of the bookcase was a wrinkled sheet of lined notebook paper with coffee stains and torn edges that Matt had respectfully saved from the trashcan.

It displayed a handwritten chastisement that self-right-eously proclaimed, "Cleanliness is next to godliness," with a happy face scribbled next to it — probably one of Thomas's wry doodlings.

In this fast-paced, high-profile company, organization-al skills required that you could find anything within a couple of minutes and still make it look like you had a heavy workload with truckloads of reading and paperwork waiting for any precious moments you could devote to them. Thomas firmly believed that he could locate any-thing he set down within three minutes. Matt and everyone else who worked with Thomas seriously doubted it. They were convinced his life and his files were in a state of con-stant disarray and that only by merciful acts of God did he get it all together in the nick of time.

Thomas never bothered to challenge them, and he did-n't openly object to someone else arranging his space. But in the past, someone else's meddling often left him in a true state of disorganization until he found where the help-ing body had put everything. Somehow he and Matt had found a kinship in their contrary styles and developed a harmonious, productive alliance.

An oversized window with an expansive view of Man-hattan made up for the lack of space. Starting to pack some take-home papers into his bag, Thomas stopped briefly to peer out the window at the city lights, then reluc-tantly returned to the pile of papers on his desk.

The muffled sound of the lobby doors swinging open announced that someone else was in the office of Holmes West, the American division of British-owned Holmes Worldwide. The most junior member of the technology applications design firm's development division, Thomas had become the product scout in America. There was plenty of potential product to check out, and he liked to do his review of Matt's research in the late hours when no one else was around. He scowled at the prospect of being interrupted again.

A shadow filled the hall outside his office, and Thomas glanced up. Philip Knight, Vice-President of Research and Development at Holmes West and the man who had recruited Thomas eighteen months ago, stopped in the doorway and leaned against it, brows raised. "Hey, buddy, you're still here? It's eight-thirty!"

Thomas frowned and played martyr to his young boss. "You're a slave driver, what can I say? I need to catch up on some things that came up the past few days while I was in Chicago."

"Hold it...not so fast, deFremond. Someday you'll appreciate the opportunities I give you, and now you're going to owe me, big time, so watch what you say until you've heard why I'm here so late too!"

"I can't wait to hear." Philip was, indeed, an ambitious workaholic, and he generally looked for a similar trait in the people he hired. He had seen that quality in Thomas, although his newest product specialist tended to be laid back, more likely to balance work with recreation. Right now Thomas longed to go home and exercise the kinks out of his muscles with a workout on the nautilus that dominated his living room.

Proudly pulling a packet of airline tickets out of his breast pocket, Philip handed them to Thomas and said, "Got a call from London, and now I've got a new project for you. I know, I know...you're just cleaning up from the Chicago trip...so I'd like you to take some time to rest up first, then meet with John Walker. Oh, that's right, you haven't met him yet, your British counterpart? Well, I'd like you to talk with him about some new marketing approaches that Malcolm is considering."

Philip beamed, clearly expecting that Thomas would jump at this opportunity.

Thomas bristled at the name "Malcolm", then scratched his chin thoughtfully and sat on the corner of his desk. He needed to be careful not to betray his distaste for the venture capitalist, whom Philip idolized. From Thomas's point of view, Malcolm Holmes epitomized cold-blooded, dehumanizing business, and Thomas struggled sometimes to rationalize working for him.

Rest up? Was this Philip speaking? He pulled the flap of the envelope open and slid the tickets out. "Philip, whoa, wait a second...these tickets are to London and Dublin! And they're for tomorrow!! Marketing's not my thing...I'm strictly development, you know that!"

"Yeah, yeah, I know. Just do this for me, will you? I can't think of anyone better for this project. It's an exciting prospect. Malcolm himself suggested we send you. And he isn't one to take no for an answer, you know. Everything's been arranged...hotel, car. A little cash to get you started. Anything else you need can be put on plastic. I want you to meet with him, Tom, and tell me what you think. Here're a few notes that Malcolm faxed over. John Walker will fill you in. He thinks these ideas can transform the company. Malcolm said something about a supermarket approach."

Philip stopped talking abruptly, looked over his shoulder, down the hall in both directions, then turned back to Thomas. In a quieter tone he said, "Then, if you've got time — no, *make* time, Tom — look into a new device that John heard about, something out of Ireland. It's not even ready yet, and nobody's listening to John — he's always off in outer space, anyway. But I'm curious about it — in fact, it's the most exciting thing I've heard in my eighteen years at Holmes. If it turns out to be anything, we might want to be there first to get it."

Philip watched Thomas as he spoke, trying to measure the impression he was making on him. "After you meet with John in England, you'll need to check it out personally in Ireland. That's where the inventor's refining it right now. He's a professor of engineering at Trinity who happens to invent things on the side...quite an extraordinary mind, from what I hear. And I want you to keep this just between us. I want your advice...if it's worth investing in, we might market it through the British store, but with an American label, too."

Shaking his head and holding up his hands in surrender, Thomas dropped the tickets on the desk and stuffed more papers into his computer bag. "Why would the Irish want to work with a British firm to market a new product? Why would I want to be a part of shoving the Brits down their throats some more? As if they haven't had enough already? This guy's in Dublin?"

Philip frowned and looked hard at Thomas. He didn't share Thomas's opinions about the centuries old history of Irish oppression by the British government. He didn't care about the past, nor did he care about a small, European country he considered to be essentially underdeveloped in technology, nor its independence, economy and political future. He was only interested in the future as it related directly to him.

"That's your job, Tom, to get the dope on what's out there for us. Anyway, he's in Cavan. I think it's somewhere on the border between Northern Ireland and the Republic. Get some R & R, you need it...but do this for us, too. This could be a whole new area for us...maybe nothing, but maybe something big. And keep this under your hat...you know how to deal with that, eh? Keep me informed by email, just be careful not to write too much detail."

Not waiting for further protest, with a quick wave Philip disappeared. Thomas stared at the space Philip had occupied. He pondered the conversation, shook his head, then finished zipping his computer bag and walked out of the office. Halfway down the hall he remembered something and jogged back to his office, where he retrieved the airline tickets and travel materials resting on top of the papers on his desk. On his way out, as he passed Matt's desk a head popped up from behind it, a pen clenched between bright white teeth. Matt was kneeling on the floor sorting through a group of files neatly laid out in a semi-circle around him. Thomas leaned over the desk and knocked on it to get Matt's attention.

"Hey! What're you doing here this late?"

"Hey," Matt responded, "I didn't even know you were here! Just finishing up a few notes on the research you asked me to do on the new Bailey model."

"That's my man. Hold down the fort for me...I'm heading for London tomorrow. Matt..." Thomas sat on the desk and looked him squarely in the eyes. Quietly, he said, "Keep your ears open for me, will you? I'll be in touch. May want your help with a new thing I'm checking out."

"Anything you need me to do now?"

"I'll let you know." Matt's gaze followed him as Thomas headed for the elevator. Recently graduated from Harvard, Matt came from a small town in upstate New York where he had graduated with honors. He had quickly made a name for himself back home when as a freshman in college he secured an internship at the White House.

Matt had intended to take a couple years off before starting law school to earn money for tuition. However, his job at Holmes working with Thomas was a stimulating break from school, and he was beginning to think he might be better suited to a career in technology development. Thomas gave Matt lots of opportunities to research and learn about technology; and the more he read, the more Matt realized how pervasive and prevalent technology was in the world. Moreover, Matt was keenly aware of how much Thomas loved his work, and the thrill of discovery was contagious. Matt watched the elevator door close and then turned back to his pile of papers.

As he pushed the down button on the elevator, Thomas sighed with confidence that he could count on Matt to back him in a host of ways...researching, contacting people, running errands, checking his business account email and replying to urgent messages when he could.

This new thing that Philip had slung at him tonight smacked of something precarious that Thomas couldn't put his finger on. And the way he commandeered Thomas's time without checking first annoyed Thomas. Hell, maybe he was just tired, but he wished he knew why this bothered him. It wasn't just his Irish freedom sympathies bugging him. The idea of a few days in Ireland was appealing to his weary soul. But, for some reason that eluded him, a sense of potential trouble lurked deep in his thoughts.

Recalling the conversation, it occurred to him that Philip's tone reminded him of the way Thomas's father frequently talked to his mother. He used a dictatorial tone to tell her that five banking associates would be coming for dinner the following evening and — he didn't say in so many words but never failed to impart the message — she should drop everything and whip up a dinner party for them. He was, after all, the breadwinner in the family and she was, with her natural talent for entertaining, expected to be there to support him.

The junior Thomas had always realized that his mother accepted Thomas Noel deFremond II's bidding and his circle of friends with mixed emotions in a contradictory, joyous animosity that puzzled him and yet increased his admiration for her.

At the age of twenty-two and following a short-lived career as a model, the Texas bred beauty of the Dallas MacKendrick clan married the tall, much-pursued bachelor descendant of a long line of French financiers. A consummate socialite, Meryl deFremond grasped opportunities to demonstrate her social refinement, at the same time easily bored by convention. Before the marriage had had a chance to mature, she had grown resentful of her husband's tiresome orders, considering herself in many ways superior to him.

Indeed, contrasting his fastidious approach to life, Meryl was dramatically spontaneous. Next to his conservative manner, his bland demeanor, and his slightly hunched posture — developed, no doubt, from years of bending over a desk reading bottomless stacks of documents — her stately presence in a room automatically attracted attention. Besides being statuesque, Meryl wore her striking auburn hair in a dramatic swept-back style that accentuated her emerald eyes. As much respect as Thomas Senior commanded for his acumen in the world of high finance, people were distracted from conversation with him when her voice could be heard across the room. People were just naturally drawn to the witty, fast-paced talk that she would so easily initiate.

Most definitely, Meryl deFremond was not a waifish

homemaker who submissively bowed to her husband's will. But she was a realist, and she knew that if it weren't for Thomas II's status among Manhattan's social and financial upper crust, her dry wit and Scottish rose beauty wouldn't suffice to attain her substantial material goals. So she bowed a little, letting him believe he was sole master of his home and family, using her manipulative powers to secure fulfillment of her own desires.

Together they were a tall, handsome couple who each, for his and her own reasons, needed to fit in with New York society. Theirs was a lackluster marriage that existed, if not ideally and lovingly synchronous, at least compatibly and to their mutual benefit. Together they bore and raised three sons, two of them just two years apart, and twelve years later, Thomas.

Meryl's defiance was regenerated in her youngest son's character, and she nurtured it enthusiastically. She would mischievously challenge him to contradict his father's wishes. When Thomas II admonished five-year-old Thomas III for his sloppy bedroom, behind the man's back Meryl winked at him and whispered, "There are more important things in life than being neat, Dodger." She nicknamed him her "Artful Dodger" in reference to their mutual efforts to elude anything akin to dull organization.

She cheered him on when as a college sophomore he declared his independence from his paternal ancestry's chosen profession and transferred from Columbia University to M.I.T. to study systems engineering. Later, when he told his parents of his intention to enter the stimulating, ever-changing arena of the computer technology industry, Meryl smugly announced the news over one of those boring bankers' dinners, much to Thomas Senior's chagrin.

Meryl was fiercely proud of her son, and her son was

fiercely loyal to her. In Thomas's mind, every girl and later every woman he met was required to meet his private set of values and qualifications before he could consider asking them to his home to meet his family. He believed that few could measure up to his mother's beauty, wisdom, wit, and strength. His affinity with his mother wouldn't be easily replaced by a relationship with another female. Consequently, he never brought dates home to meet her.

Strange...he hadn't thought about his parents in awhile, and he rarely thought about his brothers, whom he'd barely known since they had attended boarding schools and didn't live at home much after he was born. Then ten years ago, on their way home from a holiday ski trip which Thomas had begged out of, his entire family — Thomas and Meryl, Bronson and Sean and their wives and four children — had perished in a plane crash that shocked the banking world and left Thomas completely alone. Despite the sporadic nature of his contact with the rest of the family, he missed them and occasionally longed — especially at times like this — to call his mother and banter with her in the good-natured manner they uniquely shared.

* * * * * *

Thomas could describe his relationship with Philip in terms similar to the way he viewed his parents' marriage. He didn't exactly revere Philip, and he occasionally yielded to the urge to contradict and defy him. Still, he respected and acknowledged Philip's shrewdness and submitted to his orders, usually obediently if not always enthusiastically. And if he could find a way to maneuver a new product through a course of his own design while fulfilling his obligation to his boss, so much the better.

He'd check out this device, and if it proved to be worth pursuing, he'd lay the groundwork his way. Philip could simply eat dirt — unwittingly, of course.

Minutes later Thomas entered his apartment, dumped his coat and bags on the floor, and turned to the kitchen to make a sandwich. Hungrily he searched the refrigerator and cupboards and reached for a jar of peanut butter. He slabbed a generous amount on a dry slice of bread and wolfed a huge bite. It stuck to the roof of his mouth. He opened a can of warm Diet Coke. Damn, he'd forgotten to stock some in the refrigerator before he left. Taking a swig, he grimaced at the warm carbonation and resumed chewing.

He poured the Coke into a glass and reached into the freezer for ice. Carelessly, he plopped some in the glass and splashed soda onto the counter, then chomped another bite as he picked up the phone and dialed his voice-mail to get messages. Listening, deleting, saving messages, from message to message, he recorded a brief response to one message in a gooey peanut-butter voice and hung up. He sat down at his desktop computer, signed on with his subscription account name, SubDude99, ignored the mail signal, and navigated right into a chat room.

* * * * * *

Belfast, Northern Ireland

> *Go on home British Soldiers, go on home,*
> *Have you got no fucking homes of your own?*
> *For 800 years, we fought you without fear!*
> *And we will fight you for 800 more!*
>
> *If you stay British soldiers, if you stay,*
> *You'll never ever beat the IRA,*
> *For the fourteen men in Derry,*
> *Are the last that you will bury*
> *So take a trip, and leave us while you may.*
>
> *Oh we're not British, we're not Saxon, we're*
>   *not English,*
> *We're Irish, and proud we are to be,*
> *So fuck your Union Jack,*
> *We want our country back*
> *We want to see old Ireland free once more!*

An old Irish pub fight song

Maggie O'Connor hung up the public phone in the booth just outside the pub, looked at her watch, and turned to Eamon. "No answer yet, I'll have to try again in a few minutes. She must be out getting groceries or shopping."

"Well then, let's have another jar while we wait, alright, lass?" He started for the door, eager to get back to the crowd and join in the boisterous fun. He could hear the strains of *Go On Home British Soldiers*, a pub song he particularly delighted in singing, and he wanted to be one of the first to lead the refrain.

Flipping her hair behind her and bunching up her scarf around her neck, Maggie smiled brightly at Eamon and determinedly insisted, "No more, Eamon Loftus...I can't drink one more tonight! What'll my boss say if I get sloshed on Guinness my very first night here?"

Eamon pouted but said, "Alright, alright pet, don't get your knickers in a twist! Let me walk you home, right?"

Feeling light-headed, Maggie tried to walk a straight line up the sidewalk. Under the streetlights she sauntered arm in arm with Eamon, laughing and humming along with the strains of the song that tumbled out of the pub. They waved good evening to a couple who leaned against the open door, exchanging quips with friends across the street. She was on the edge between feeling silly but not quite tipsy.

Spotting their bed and breakfast, they stopped in the middle of the street, looked at each other, and burst into laughter again. Inside the well-lit foyer, they were greeted by Eamon's English Springer spaniel, Morgan, who enthusiastically bounded across the hall to greet his master and slobbered a wet licking tongue on his hands.

Maggie waved hello to their hosts, Reggie and Violet Williamson, who sat in the parlor watching television. She had warmed to their hospitality quickly, but she also surmised that they were Scottish-descended Protestants who held thinly disguised opinions about their religious faction's superiority. They referred proudly to Northern Ireland as part of the Commonwealth. She had immediately seized the opportunity to hear their point of view about the still-delicate discord among Belfast's opposing inhabitants, and they accommodated her willingly.

Coming from the darkness outside into the bright foyer light had sobered Maggie. She said goodnight to Eamon and the Williamsons and sprinted up the stairs to her room on the second floor. She set her purse on the dresser, unbuttoned her jacket and hung it neatly over a chair.

Stepping back into the hallway to a phone just outside her door, Maggie called her boss in Minneapolis. As it rang, she stared at her jacket, carried the phone with the long cord dragging behind her and straightened the jacket so the shoulders hung squarely on the chair. Satisfied, she returned her attention to the ringing. His answering machine picked up, so she recorded a message, "George, I'm here in Belfast...did you get my notes? Let me know what you think about the introduction. Tomorrow I'm doing the town. Hey! Thanks loads for arranging the Irish videographer...Eamon's a charm...I think. Later, George." Frowning, she started to chastise herself for calling him after downing those mugs of stout, then decided what the hell.

Maggie, thirty-eight years old, single, on her second career after giving up teaching in a small Catholic school in a poor inner city neighborhood of Minneapolis, was grateful to George for having had faith in her. An English major at St. Catherine's, she had graduated with a teaching certificate and a zealous mission to transform her first class of seventh grade students into literary connoisseurs. In the meantime, she had put on hold her own passion, writing.

After fifteen years teaching in a stifling square classroom of pale green block walls, where she daily faced the challenge of steering adolescent hormones in a scholarly direction, her restless nature longed for change. It didn't help matters that her three-year relationship with Joe Wright had ended bitterly last summer. She felt lonely at times, needing more than drifting seventh grade minds and other stressed out teachers for company.

Fortuitously, a classroom project involving a visiting editor from Toulouse Productions provided an opportunity for her to make her escape. She had written to Toulouse, a small but widely respected production company that specialized in travel documentaries, requesting a presentation to her class during a descriptive writing unit they were studying. On a whim she had enclosed an article she had written about houseboating along the Mississippi River bluffs that had been published in the St. Paul Pioneer Press travel section. The visiting editor stayed after class and joined Maggie in the faculty room for lunch. He had indeed read her article and recognized a potential in her, suggesting she apply at Toulouse for an opening they had posted for a documentary journalist.

Here she was, already on her third major assignment from George, who had wanted her to start the day he interviewed her but reluctantly agreed that she should finish out the school year. One of her first assignments, a trek across the Canadian Rockies, had exhilarated her body and soul, stimulated her mind, and convinced her she'd made the right decision. George had been pleased, but he wasn't one to lavish praise. Let the writers' academy commend his staff with awards. He rewarded them with what motivated them most: desirable projects.

Back in October, in his gruff, brusque manner, he had summoned Maggie to his office.

"You did a good job, Maggie," he'd said. "After we get a few short projects out of the way, I'd like you to go to Ireland in the spring. Do a documentary on the movement of Irish-Americans back to Ireland."

Maggie was ecstatic. "Ireland? George! Wow, I'd love to. What's your angle?"

"I want you to contrast rural and urban Ireland with America. Focus on the Irish initiative to move people from the inner city back out to rural parts of the country as well as to attract Irish Americans back to their ancestral homeland. Their incentive is farmland homesteading. I want to inject another twist — a segment about the socioeconomic differences between urban and rural life in Northern Ireland and the Republic."

"Intriguing," she said. "But why wait till spring? Why not December?"

"December? Nah, I've been there in December. Everything's wet and cold and gloomy. December's a time for snow and places that are festive...you know, holiday places like New England. Ireland should be filmed in spring and summer, when everything's green and flowery and such."

"Wait now, George, think about it. You're right, nobody thinks about Ireland in wintertime. So with a story coming out in February, we'd be a jump ahead of other production companies that might be planning to do something on Ireland."

"Nah, I don't see it."

"Well, look at it this way. By researching the story during a season when tourism is light, I'll have a better chance of capturing the natural qualities of the country in the documentary. I could show it more like it is in everyday life. Isn't that what you want?"

He was hard to convince. "We have to satisfy the network that commissioned us. They don't want to see drab landscapes and people who are ornery because their houses are freezing cold and the sun hasn't shined in weeks."

Maggie paused, weighing quickly whether she should

risk offending her boss. When debating an issue, she tended to jump in and say what she was thinking without first considering the consequences. She trusted her instincts, though. She slumped in her chair and rolled her eyes up toward the ceiling, folding her arms in front of her.

"Hmmm...I had this idea I was working for a company that does realistic, issue-based documentaries about cultures and politics and history. You're kind of making this sound more like a travelogue."

That did it. George hated it when Toulouse Productions was equated with travelogue companies. He disdained those kinds of productions, calling them "vanity films." He had contemptuously quit his job with a production company when it shifted from educational videos to films that would have wider market penetration. But he loved his chosen career, so he started his own company, targeting his productions to people who watched them for intellectual investigation more than entertainment. He was his own boss.

But he still had to please the networks that bought his productions. He rubbed his massive hands over his wrinkled, balding head, scowled, and looked across his desk at Maggie skeptically.

"You're a good writer, but you're a novice researcher. I want this documentary to get into the economics, the politics, the issues between rural and urban, North and South, touch on the history, go in-depth into the character of the people and on top of all that, make it look beautiful to watch. You think you can do that with a winter story?"

"Absolutely," she said with certainty. "I can do it. It'll be better than a spring one. I'll find a way to correlate the season and the weather with the issues."

"Okay," he shrugged, then added in his gruffest tone,

"I'll expect you to make it the best one we've done. But get your other jobs out of the way first." It wasn't a warning, but Maggie knew it was a challenge. That was George's way of letting people know he'd been won over.

During the next few days, they outlined the documentary she would pursue over the coming weeks. Maggie would begin her story with a brief account of the emigration of Irish families to America. Then she would review the Irish government's efforts to reverse the process, a strategy intended to modernize Ireland's industry, boosted by American resourcefulness and ingenuity.

Maggie had another, personal motive for doing the story in Ireland as soon as possible — getting away from Joe and stinging memories of the secret aspects of their relationship. It was something she kept to herself, like other, deeper secrets from her childhood, except for confidences shared with her sister Jane, who knew her secrets and thus understood her ways better than anyone else. The rest of her family, along with all their mutual friends, had been ignorant of Joe's abusive tendencies, something he skillfully concealed behind a mask of gregarious congeniality. Right or wrong, she had no urge to correct everyone's incomplete and erroneous perception of him.

Doing the story afforded Maggie another opportunity, a personal quest that had been evolving in her head for years. Beginning in the sixth grade she had listened to her great-uncle Francis O'Connor weave tales about his childhood in southeast Ireland and his claim to direct descent from the High King Rory O'Connor. Colorful visions of the high rolling hills of Tara, where throngs of Celts congregated to honor their brave king at the post looking out across vast Irish meadowlands, filled Maggie's head and fueled her dream to go there one day and behold it herself.

Perhaps she could capture a piece of the mystical charm that belonged to the Irish. She didn't know she already possessed it.

* * * * * *

Another glance at her watch, and Maggie once again dialed her younger sister Jane in Minnetonka to check in.

"Hello, Pratts," Jane answered as she unzipped her jacket, hit the button to close the garage door, and looked out the window at the swirling snow building drifts along her driveway. *Looks like a hot cocoa and peppermint schnapps night*, she mused.

"Jane, I made it...long, long flight, got re-routed through London, but I'm in one piece. Already had my first Guinness!"

Covering the phone, Jane yelled behind her, "Charlie! It's Aunt Mag. She's there!" She turned back to the phone. "Just one Guinness? Right. Honey, I'd give anything to trade places with you right now. I miss you already! I just got home from stocking up on groceries. We've got another storm coming in. It's eight inches deep outside already, and we're expecting five more and high winds overnight."

"Well, I don't miss the snow right now, but I think I'm gonna miss it on Christmas Eve. Save some in the freezer for me, will you? I have to get in one good snowball fight with Charlie before winter's over."

Charlie picked up another extension. "Hey, Magpie, you got a hookup?"

"Yes, sweetie...I'm all set...got my adapter, got a plug...we're loaded and ready to fire away!"

"Then hang up and let's get online!"

Jane put a halt to the notion. "Charlie, you've got homework! Besides, it probably costs a fortune over there to chat online!"

"I gotta go, Jane...just wanted to check in with you, let you know everything's a-okay."

"Love you, hon. Stay in touch every few days, okay? I promised Mom. Oh Maggie! Joe called here looking for you."

Maggie winced at the mention of her ex. "Joe? Joe who? Honestly, Jane, it's been six months. I thought he accepted that it's over. It took me a long time to end it with him."

"I know, honey, I know. Don't worry about it, I doubt he'll call again. Take care over there, will you, Maggie? I love you!"

"Love you too, Jaybird. And yes I'll be careful. Tell Mom I'm fine and I'll call her. Later."

Turning to her laptop, Maggie logged on with her online address EZWriter, checked her mail, then entered a chat room. Perched cross-legged on her bed, feeling flirty, she watched the dialogue scroll down her screen with fast and furious bantering.

She had discovered online chatting only a few months before and found she enjoyed the anonymity. It intrigued her to talk with people she might never see, and she liked the idea that physical appearance could play little or no part in becoming acquainted. In fact, she determinedly refused to describe herself to others, and if they wanted to continue to visit with her online, they had to accept this as her rule.

Still giddy from the extra pint, amused by the multitude of senseless conversations simultaneously crossing her screen, she read some of the dialogue aloud to herself, trying out the lines in a different voice for each person she was "reading." She began typing in response...

Cottonwood: ANY HOT LADIES IN HERE WANT TO CYBER IM ME.

SubDude99: Cotton, NEVER get online and go into a room and in all caps say....

Cheszarr: Dancing

SubDude99: ANY HOT LADIES IN HERE WANT TO CYBER IM ME NOW!!!!!

SubDude99: Right ladies?

Cottonwood: you mean it only works half the time?

EZWriter: Subtle, SubDude, very subtle.

Cheszarr: Only if you are half assed, Cotton.

SubDude99: Not me, EZ! I was telling Cotton not to say that!

EZWriter: Wow, chivalrous romantics! My kind of place.

SubDude99: Thanks EZ! LOL

Cheszarr: Champagne, strawberries, chocolate and dancing...now that's romantic.

EZWriter: Speaking of chocolate...

SubDude99: yes pure Swiss chocolate that melts even before you taste it

EZWriter: I found the niftiest chocolate...

SubDude99: tell us about the chocolate EZ

EZWriter: Tobler, chocolate orange...shaped like an orange, and when you whack it on the table....

EZWriter: it comes apart in slices like an orange. Scrumptious!

Cheszarr: EZ, my mom got one of those oranges for Christmas...wouldn't share.

SubDude99: chocolate and a whack on the table...?

SandyDee02: YMMMM

SubDude99: Sounds violent.

EZWriter: Only for a second, just a bang to crack it open, then you spread the wedges apart and begin to enjoy.

SubDude99: you realize chocolate releases endorphins?

EZWriter: Absolutely. That's the point. Sometimes you have to inflict a little pain to feel a little joy.

SubDude99: A philosopher!

Grinning, Maggie leaped off the bed to answer a light knock on her door. She found no one there, but a tray of tea and biscuits had been set outside her room. She looked down the hallway and caught a shadow in the stairwell.

"Violet?"

"Aye, Girl, din't mean to interrupt. I sees ye're busy on yere baby computer."

"Well, no bother, but anyway, thanks for the tea!"

"Aye, sleep well, dear."

Maggie chuckled at Violet's term for her laptop. Grabbing a cookie and pouring a cup of tea, she daintily sat back down on the narrow bed, taking care not to tip her laptop over the edge. She looked at the screen and said, "Damn!" The screen had frozen and a message appeared at the top:

"THIS TEMPORARY PROBLEM WILL BE
RESOLVED SHORTLY.
IN THE MEANTIME TRY IM'S."

"Now what?" she asked no one out loud. She was

answered with a light jingling and another dialogue box on her monitor.

> **SubDude99**: giving it a try...no chat...said to try Instant Messages.

Amused to hear from one of her "roommates", she responded.

> **EZWriter**: This is like the lights going out in a storm!

> **SubDude99**: My screen froze in the middle of a sentence, just when I could start to taste one of those oranges.

> **EZWriter**: LOL! What a drag...just when you find a fun room.

> **SubDude99**: yes rare.

> **SubDude99**: I am a sucker for technology, though...unlike the naysayers, I think chat rooms are just another brainchild of the techno-wizards that makes the world smaller in terms of communications.

> **EZWriter**: I agree.

> **SubDude99**: Where you at, EZ?

> **EZWriter**: Now, or usually?

> **SubDude99**: A cryptic, eh? Or just plain old avoidance? Anyway, I'm headed for Europe tomorrow for a few weeks.

> **EZWriter**: Hey! Europe! I'm a sucker for any part of the world...love to travel...

> **EZWriter**: Business or pleasure?

> **SubDude99**: A little of both...might do some writing while I'm over there...

> **EZWriter**: Writing?

SubDude99: poetry, short stories, that sort of stuff...nothing serious.

EZWriter: whoa, poetry? I'm a traveling journalist for documentaries.

SubDude99: a real writer!!! professional? and yes, poetry.

EZWriter: aye...my best story, I think, was a trek across part of Canada last year, from the Rockies to Winnipeg.

SubDude99: I could send you one of my short stories...interested?

EZWriter: Absolutely! Thought you'd never offer.

SubDude99: but you must send me one of yours. And understand, spelling and grammar are not high on my list of priorities. Hey, about that chocolate orange thing...

EZWriter: Yes?

SubDude99: What you said about sometimes you have to feel pain to get joy?

EZWriter: Something like that.

SubDude99: Well, if someone were going to crack you open, get to your deepest feelings, would that be tough for you? Would it hurt?

EZWriter: Are you sure you're not a psychiatrist? That sounds like a psychiatrist kind of question to me.

SubDude99: Just curious.

Maggie jumped, remembering to check her watch. Realizing the lateness and recalling her ambitious plans for the next day, it was time to cut off this silliness. But he was sort of interesting, this fellow writer... She looked up his profile, found his first name and his location, and saved it in a file.

> **EZWriter**: Have to go now, Thomas. I'll be waiting for that story.
>
> **SubDude99**: Wait!! Hey...EZ?
>
> **EZWriter**: Laddie, ye'll be the death of me! It's way past me bedtime!
>
> **SubDude99**: Bedtime? You work odd hours?
>
> **EZWriter**: Would ye have me missin' me beauty rest, lad? Shame on ye! {{{***}}}

With that, Maggie signed off abruptly, leaving Thomas perplexed. Who was this lady? Quickly, before he forgot it, Thomas grabbed a pencil and paper and wrote down her screen name. He looked up her profile:

Member Profile - EZWRITER

Name: Margaret (Maggie to friends and close relations

Location: Minnesota

Gender: guess

Occupation: Writer, see

  www.toulouseproductions.com.

Favorite Quote: Silently, one by one, in the infinite meadows of heaven, blossomed the lovely stars, the forget-me-nots of the angels. Longfellow

He smiled. Her name — Maggie. Ha! And she knew his name! She must have found it in his profile while they were talking.

Maggie did the same. Reopening the file she'd saved, she read the rest of his profile:

Member Profile — SUBDUDE99

Name: Thomas

Location: NYC

Gender: Last I checked...

Occupation: Product development, technology industry

Favorite Quote: Stop and consider! Life is but a day; a fragile dew-drop on its perilous way from a tree's summit; a poor Indian's sleep while his boat hastens to the monstrous steep of Mont Morenci. Keats

Thomas. Thomas? She pondered the name, attempting to put a face to the name. *What kind of a man would be named Thomas?*

"Thomas...Thomas...Thomas," she recited out loud to try out the name with her voice. Nice, but sort of Biblical and formal sounding, she decided. She knew several guys named Tom and none of them went by their given name. She stared at his quote, thinking hard, trying to picture this person at the other end of the conversation the same way she tried with other people she met online. Probably tall, dark, extremely handsome and way out of her league. Either that or — more likely — very ugly and way shorter than her.

Another thought interrupted her wondering. *Whoa. I'm breaking my own rule,* she thought, *I've got to stop this.* And she was glad to note he hadn't once asked her what she looked like. She turned her musing back to his profile.

Keats...he does like poetry...a guy wouldn't use a quote like that unless he was into poetry. She gave up and closed the file. She started to shut down her computer and close the laptop lid. Then, on impulse, she reopened it, waited while the program launched, and wrote an email to her new acquaintance, attaching a file that contained her Canadian journals.

To: SubDude99

From: EZWriter

> *Okay, Thomas, ready for some torture? I didn't say I was enthralling, but here's some bedtime reading that if nothing else should help you sleep. Thanks for the chin wagging, Thomas...you're nice. ;-) Maggie*

She read it back to herself out loud, then straightened up and addressed her reflection in the mirror over the dressing table, "What are you, nuts?" She thought a moment, frowned, then sent it anyway.

* * * * * *

Thomas sat back and half-smiled, revitalized by the pleasure of his conversation with the stranger called EZWriter. Rarely did he feel any commonality with a fellow "cyber cruiser," as the aficionados called themselves. The ladies he met this way remained casual acquaintances if anything, someone to say hello to, to carry on light conversation, to share a brief human connection.

He kept telling himself he should only carry on extensive conversations with "real" friends and avoid these long distance acquaintances. Frequently he heard about people who met and married through a chance encounter online. The people in these rooms, although sometimes amusing and occasionally interesting, were also often recent victims of failed relationships or widowed. Sometimes they were borderline nymphomaniacs who couldn't spell "nymphomaniac," much less define it. Then there were the nice women who always lived thousands of miles away.

This woman, though...he liked her immediately and he wanted to ignore his misgivings. He didn't understand the attraction, nor did he care to analyze it...it was more than mild amusement, more uplifting than anything he'd experienced the past few years, so why question it? He was intrigued. He wondered what she looked like. Best not to ask, at least not right away, he'd learned from watching other chat room conversations.

To maintain his optimism about love and romance, Thomas constantly reminded himself of the adage that if one wants something badly enough one will find a way to get it. It had been almost three years since Clarese walked out of his life. They had lived together for a long time, off and on, having met in a coffee shop on Seventh Avenue near Central Park where she worked as a waitress.

On an impulse he gave her a five-dollar tip for serving him a cup of coffee with a smile. He had seen that she must be new and wanted to make her day...nothing more than that. As he sat there finishing his coffee and reading his notes from the day, she sidled over and hovered, patiently waiting for him to look up and then asking if there was anything else she could get for him.

He had been amused, not wanting anything else or considering that he might meet her again. When he left he caught the look on her face — the perfect expression of *thank you* and *why did you do that* and *come hither* all mixed together, and that was enough for him.

A week later, they met again as he meandered along a sidewalk art fair. Alone and a little lonely, he had just bought a hot dog and wanted to quickly free his hands to read the fair flyer, so he stuffed the hot dog into his mouth to hold it as he turned the pages of the flyer. Walking around the corner of a booth, he blindly bumped into Clarese while critiquing an ink drawing that looked to him somewhat childish yet promising, an image of a family picnicking in the park.

"You're looking at my drawing," she had said, hopeful of a potential sale, and then brightened with recognition when he looked up at her.

It hadn't lasted, however, as hard as they tried. Despite his adventurous spirit, he couldn't keep her entertained. Her gypsy soul sent her wandering further and further away, searching for something he couldn't give her because he didn't know what she wanted.

Returning his thoughts to the present, Thomas smiled with satisfaction...he felt as if he had just received his five-dollar tip back.

chapter 3

INVENTION AND DISCOVERY

D r. Ian Pennton worked alone in his lab, which filled the small stone shed behind his thatched-roof cottage outside of Belturbet, not far south of the Republic-Northern Ireland border. He stretched, coughed, pulled his sweater closer about him, and never moved his eyes off the object before him. On the radio behind him, Terri Taconawa sang a Brazillian ballad that sounded like an exotic derivation of Celtic music.

The old scientist perched on a rickety bar stool at a thick wooden bench, toying with four small plates of glass. The cramped, brightly lit room boasted sophisticated apparata used in an etching process; negatives of lithos hung on a line with clothespins; bottles of acid were carefully labeled in neat handwriting. Shelves of computers in various stages of disassembly lined the walls. Some machines were bared of their outer casings, revealing their guts. Tangled cables and keyboards were stacked high and dangling over the edge of a decrepit wheelcart.

One computer, scrupulously clean and whole, rested on a table behind the professor, furiously feeding endless scrolls of scientific equations across the monitor as if it were running a search for the ultimate answer of the meaning of life as a mathematical model. Mechanical gadgets dominated the huge work bench in the center of the lab.

Some devices looked like cryogenic tanks. Smooth, shiny, frost-covered cylinders rested deathly still in fish-tank-like glass enclosures. In the center of one tank sat a turntable apparatus with a remote arm that appeared to be controlled with a joystick and connected to another computer device. It was designed very basically for spinning the glass plates. Under the right conditions a super thin metallic crystal of startling properties could be forced to form on the glass plate.

No one would ever have surmised, looking at that centuries old homestead surrounded by its hip-high stone wall set right up against the narrow country road, that its simple shed housed a genius mind and an invention that could impact Ireland's economy. Nobody, looking at the slight frame and the white wispy hair of the elderly man hunched over his work at the table, would have guessed that his brain held the genius that could make the invention work.

Dr. Pennton saw nothing but the parts before him, diligently studying the mechanism he designed to align sheets of glass. He picked up the small dictator, checked his note pad, and began to speak.

"Alignment trial number 879. Laser alignment of the registration mark in the center eliminated the need to realign the sheets mechanically. I have set the four sheets into a simple mechanical frame with no adjustment devices...just a set screw."

With painstaking precision, Pennton adjusted the sandwiched sheets of six inch glass squares to form a screen of sorts in a metal frame. In front of the quarter-inch thick "screen," a three-dimensional image crudely displayed a toy top in color. The professor tightened one of the setscrews which held the frame together and the image became clear. It was a spinning top which began to wobble on its axis and then fell on its side.

He pressed a button on one of the keyboards and the top began to spin again, radiating bands of bright colors. Elated, he deemed the trial a success and picked up the object, sheets of plate glass only one quarter inch thick held together with a black metal frame that had a tiny ribbon cable attached to one side. Tenderly, he placed the frame on a stand to position it vertically in front of him, like a regular computer monitor.

Kathleen Pennton opened the shed door and stepped inside, carrying a tray with tea and biscuits. Seeing the triumph on her husband's face, she smiled with pleasure. Quietly she set the tray down and watched him continue to dictate.

"Alignment trial number 879 is a success. Note: Use a finer adjustment screw with a shorter length, possibly restricted to quarter turn either direction." He clicked the dictator off and swiveled the bar stool around to reach his arms out to her.

"It's goin' good then, is it, Ian?"

"Aye, girl. I've got it! Come here now, your timin' is impeccable. Let's have a hug and a celebration toast."

Kathleen laughed and gladly embraced him, giving him a kiss on the top of his head. He patted her smooth, silver-threaded hair, then cupped her face in his hands and kissed her long and deeply. She poured the tea and they gazed at each other with victorious relief, holding up their cups in toast to the flat screen device.

This elderly couple had never known romantic love other than what they felt for each other. As small children reared on neighboring farms, they were inseparable playmates. They were both baptized and confirmed in Stag Hall Catholic Church, and after growing up together, they were married there, too.

Kathleen's increasing depression over remaining childless for the first ten years of their marriage was replaced with joyful expectancy when she became pregnant. But she lost the child seven months into her pregnancy. Ian's constant and unswerving love eventually did what no one else — friends, doctors, the parish priest — could to coax her out of the despair she suffered.

They lavished the love they had been saving up for their unborn child on nieces and nephews who visited them frequently. Kathleen's nurturing and generous nature and Ian's playfulness were beloved by their friends and neighbors across County Cavan. Throughout their life together, which spanned close to three-quarters of a century, they grew closer and closer, until one could finish the other's sentences, one would often know what the other was thinking from a look or a movement, a spoken word or silence. Sometimes she would blurt out a laugh before he had completed half of a witty comment, and if she was annoyed by something he'd done, she'd finish his apology for him. Then he'd mutter, "For once, woman, could I at least say a whole 'sorry' to the very end?" and they'd both stop short and laugh, his offense forgotten.

Kathleen shared Ian's triumph with the device, experiencing exactly the same tingle across her flesh that he did, feeling flushed with the same warmth flowing through her veins as he.

"This is it, then, love," he said quietly, feeling the full jubilation, the endless hours of effort and disappointment, of trials and failures, of finally succeeding. It was one of the rare times when his ideas were solidly validated. For this moment he didn't care that it just seemed to come together all by itself. As almost always happened, the answer would soon register and he'd know what he did this time that was different from all the other attempts. What mattered was that it was working. He could come back to it later and figure out why. It was working. "Cheers!"

* * * * * *

Belfast, Northern Ireland

Sometime around three a.m. Maggie was aroused from a deep sleep to the clear-pitched, poignant sound of someone whistling the melody to her old favorite American movie, *Casablanca*. Drifting in and out of subconsciousness to measures of *As Time Goes By*, her sleep was interrupted again minutes later by the loud, dissonant voices of students returning home from an all-nighter. "Everyone sings here!" she groaned and drifted off again.

That morning Maggie and Eamon found their hosts bustling between the kitchen and the box-shaped dining room. Reggie and Violet were delighted to have guests during this slow time of year in Belfast and insisted on pampering the American and her camera-toting Irish sidekick with a full breakfast served traditional Irish style.

Violet brought tea and then closed the door to the kitchen, but before she did, Reggie saw Maggie shivering, apparently unaccustomed to the lack of central heating. Within a few minutes he had located a small, hardly used space heater in the storage room of the big, four-story house and placed it in the dining room next to the side-board where the family china was carefully arranged on top of fine lace linen.

Gratefully, Maggie leaned down to rub her hands by the heat, then sat back upright as Violet entered with steaming plates of eggs, rashers, fried tomatoes, and soda bread. Chattering away, asking about their comfort and hoping they'd rested well, she poured tea, replaced the cloth tea warmer, and, still chattering away, left the room and closed the door once again to give them privacy.

"Well, pet," said Eamon, "we've got the whole day in Belfast...where would you like to go first?"

Maggie finished a bite and replied, "I want to see it all, Eamon...but first take me to Shankill and Falls Road."

"Ah, pet, why do you want to go there first? Looking for the dirt, are ye?"

"No, not at all!" she protested, "I told you, I'm not into politics...just want to see the city from every perspec-tive...will you help me do that?"

Eamon set down his fork and wiped his mouth with a linen napkin. "You don't understand, Maggie. It's danger-ous in some parts. It's been quiet for a spell now, but the underground factions are constantly provoking each other. You can be walking up what seems a perfectly quiet street, and suddenly you're surrounded by gunfire. I'll grant you it happens rarely, but that's the terror of it...you never know when the violence will start up again."

"I do understand, Eamon. But if I go through life avoid-ing this hazard and that, pretty soon my life will be over and I'll have seen and done nothing! I'm not looking for trouble, but I want to see where the Troubles took place."

Eamon studied her for a few seconds, then took a long breath and gave in. A stubborn colleen she was; clearly he'd lost this argument before it began. He picked up his fork again and fell silent. Realizing she'd get her way, Maggie took a large gulp of juice and wisely said no more.

Minutes later, their breakfast finished and their equipment stowed in bags hanging from straps slung diagonally across their shoulders, they stepped outside into the soft air of an almost imperceptible mist. They hiked past a long row of red brick townhouses on Eglantine Road toward Malone, armed with umbrellas, notebook and cameras. They stopped at Queen's University, strolling through the Botanic Gardens, then through Ulster Museum for a thorough lesson on Northern Ireland history, industry, and culture. Maggie made notes about things she wanted to research more and asked Eamon questions about several items she noticed in the museum.

Later, as they reached the City Centre, Maggie spotted a strange looking vehicle that resembled an army tank and asked Eamon about it.

"That's an armor-plated Land Rover — RUC," he explained, "Don't point, Maggie, and for the love o' Jesus, don't take photos of them....if they see you, they'll take your film....and for pity's sakes, don't hum the Republic anthem!" Piqued by his relentless bossiness and his arrogance, Maggie resolved to break a few of Eamon's "rules".

Entering City Centre through the gates that would close it off within seconds if violence should erupt, they wandered down streets swarming with shoppers. Maggie stopped to chat with shopkeepers and members of the Royal Ulster Constabulary (despite Eamon's continual admonitions), captivated by the hard-edged Irish brogue punctuated with a notable Scottish influence. She and Eamon spent the day walking around Belfast, twice hailing taxis to give their feet a rest, shooting roll after roll and video of the city's architecture and its people...groups of school children in uniform, black cabs with their distinctive low rumble and cramped front seats, thick crowds of pedestrians, street vendors, City Hall and government buildings. They crossed a walking bridge past the Prince Andrew Clock Tower to H & W Shipbuilding, where Eamon pointed out the derrick at which the Titanic had been constructed.

Stopping for a lunch of thick Irish stew at Copperfield's, Maggie pulled out her notepad and scribbled some notes.

* * * * * *

Journal Entry — Belfast.

Belfast is a bustling town with a mixed complexion of contemporary and old-world buildings, cosmopolitan and small town at once with its shops, churches, and people. On street corners you'll find vendors selling cheap junk, calling out long, unintelligible phrases that always end, "...only a pound!" We've feasted on Irish stew, and while I've enjoyed a mug of Irish coffee, Eamon has quenched his thirst on a foamy long draw of Guinness. The city is fascinating, boiling with energy, youth and emotion.

College students here are quite boisterous (throughout the entire night!) but are courteous, clean cut, neat...the City Centre is litter-free. As we stroll down residential blocks, cars honk as if they were in the downtown area maneuvering through heavy traffic. But I've discovered that my obvious American apparel has given me away, and the honks aren't to complain about traffic but

*rather are friendly teasing from the locals, who
laugh and wave as they pass me by.*

* * * * * *

She closed her notebook and looked at Eamon as he
chewed a last forkful of stew.

"Eamon," she cooed, sugar-sweetly, "Take me to the
other places now, the places where tourists don't go."
Frowning, Eamon reluctantly stood and led her up the
street toward the places he didn't like to go for the memories they evoked.

Under his watchful eye, she photographed evidence of
the too recent Troubles and barraged him with questions
about the peace wall, the barbed wire along the roof of the
RUC compounds, the murals, the symbols painted here
and there. Writing furiously in brief phrases, hoping she
wouldn't forget any details, Maggie translated her notes
that evening on her laptop.

* * * * * *

Journal Entry — Belfast, the Troubles.

*Today we ventured into areas where tourists
are unlikely to walk alone, so soon after the Troubles have been proclaimed at rest, although who
knows for how long, really.*

*We wandered around the Protestant downtown, where militant murals on building walls cry
out their impassioned proclamations, where the
Union Jack flies high, and where barbed wire
skirts the tops of brick walls. There the curbs are*

painted red, white and blue, and all around there is evidence of the recent conflicts.

Up into the Catholic neighborhood — the Falls — we hiked, then through an opening in the miles-long, twenty-foot high "peace wall" into Shankill, the Protestant side, and back down the streets of everyday Belfast.

You can't miss the tell-tale signs of the now-suppressed conflicts...buildings with big gaping holes in their walls that are now being refurbished after bombings, new murals painted — probably in honor of President Clinton's recent visit — depicting an attempt toward tolerance, as moving as the older murals proclaiming Ulster will never fall under Irish rule!

We walked through a shabby neighborhood in the Falls Road area, where the streets abut block-long apartment buildings with windows bricked over, into Corpus Christi Church with its ornate walls, altar, and woodwork, very old but very reverently preserved...then through Percy Place, the acknowledged breeding grounds for militants, where murals appear more frequently and portray hooded soldiers brandishing machine guns. We've been warned to shoot our footage quickly and then hold the camera and recorder down at our sides while walking so the RUC won't confiscate our film.

In the Protestant area near the "peace wall," the Sinn Fein headquarters is thinly disguised as a bookshop. There a man approached us; he seemed to be staggering. I suspected him to be a drunken derelict looking for a handout. However, he asked for nothing, simply inquired where we were from, shook our hands, and welcomed us to his city.

Thus we're reminded that people who depend solely on the news media for their impressions of a conflict-torn country will never enjoy a full, well-rounded appreciation of the gentle, gregarious people behind the conflict and the culture that leads some to drown their tension in drink.

* * * * * *

An alarm sounded on her computer, and Maggie recalled her promise to make a connection with Charlie. She signed on, expecting to find him waiting for her, but she got there first and used the opportunity to check her mail. Soon Charlie's screen name popped up on her monitor.

PratBrat:: Waving finger:: Tisk, tisk, tisk...always online!

EZWriter: If you're catching me online....so must you be? (tsk, tsk, waving back!)

PratBrat: heheh...well, yeah...My mom is mad I spent 21 hours online last month..I can't help it, I'm a kid of the future...ya' know!

EZWriter: you need the $19.95 special, Charlie...

PratBrat: They won't pay the "$19.95 special..."

EZWriter: They're paying more than that when you're on 21 hours!

PratBrat: Yeah... I Know!!

EZWriter: Charlie, could you do me a favor? Could you call Grandma and tell her for me I did NOT make it to Great Aunt Hilda's funeral...not enough time before my trip over here.

EZWriter: Grandma's probably miffed with me...

PratBrat: Oh, well, she's here talking to Mom....telling her now.

EZWriter: ...and I lost track of time at Barnes & Noble...

EZWriter: I get lost in myself when I'm in that bookstore...

EZWriter: they should put a cot and pillow in the back room for me...

EZWriter: Is she mad?

PratBrat: Naw. Heheh....Lotsa books. Learn to read real fast, and you'll never have to pay for a book again.

Suddenly a signal popped up and an instant message filled a corner of her screen.

SubDude99: Hey! Maggie!!

She returned the greeting and said goodbye to Charlie.

EZWriter: Business is calling, Charlie...Please tell your Mom I'm fine, okay?

PratBrat: Ok, have fun, Magpie...

EZWriter: Gotta go, sweetie...

EZWriter: Love ya! XOXOXOX

PratBrat: Kisses!!! Aaaarrrgggh

EZWriter: (grinning)

* * * * * *

London, same time

Thomas had arrived in London and had his bags open, clothes strewn about his hotel room, briefcase and computer on the desk by the window, and stacks of papers piled on the table. Pouring a cup of coffee brought up by room service, he yawned and looked out the window at London's evening lights. Jetlagged but anxious to maintain communications with Matt, he set up his laptop and signed online to find a brief message from Philip and a signal that EZ Writer was online.

Back in Belfast, Maggie's door to her bedroom was open to the main hallway. Waiting for her to join him for supper, Eamon paced back and forth past her door, checking his watch every few seconds. He had no time for computers, much less the Internet and all its strange wizardry.

Something in Eamon's attitude about the Internet warned Maggie not to tell him she was talking with a stranger online. She didn't want to rankle him, nor receive another lecture so soon after their tour of the war-torn areas of Belfast. She explained with a white lie, "I'll just be another minute, Eamon. I'm talking to my nephew."

He stopped in front of her door. "Well then, I'll meet you downstairs, okay, love?"

She just nodded. Her attention was riveted to the screen.

EZWriter: Hello, Thomas.

SubDude99: Terrific story on Canada!

EZWriter: You read it already?

SubDude99: Didn't want to wait. You're pretty good.

EZWriter: Thanks, Chief (smiling). Now when are you going to reciprocate?

SubDude99: Ah, such a fine new acquaintance requires a special piece. Let me think on it, okay?

EZWriter: Okay.

SubDude99: Enjoyed meeting you the other night. But you didn't tell me much about yourself!

EZWriter: You first.

SubDude99: I am handsome with blue eyes and a dazzling smile.

EZWriter: Ugh.

SubDude99: Sorry. That's not what you meant, eh?

EZWriter: I know that you're from New York City...where?

EZWriter: and you work with computers somehow....

EZWriter: and that you read Keats. Wow, that quote ....you ARE a guy, right? (grinning)

SubDude99: (looking down) yes, guy, absolutely. I like Keats.

SubDude99: Manhattan. And I know that....

SubDude99: you're in Minneapolis....

SubDude99: and a writer...

SubDude99: and you like Longfellow...nice quote yourself, Maggie.

EZWriter: What else does one need to know?

SubDude99: How do you like your coffee in the morning?

EZWriter: Served on a tray in bed. And I prefer tea, with scones, a jar of preserves, butter...not one of those containers I can't open but on the side...

EZWriter: in a pretty little china dish.

SubDude99: picky!

SubDude99: Would a mug do?

EZWriter: In a pinch. If you deliver it. But don't forget the cloth napkin.

SubDude99: You mean I should get up first and make the tea?

EZWriter: Only if you know how to brew it properly. And go out and buy fresh scones every morning. Or you could get up really early and make them. (LOL)

SubDude99: Do I gather correctly that you are spoiled?

EZWriter: No but I would like to be, now that you ask. I am hard working, driven to excel...determined...charming....a terrific dancer. What else would you like to know?

SubDude99: Music. What kind of music do you listen to?

Smiling at their silliness, Maggie looked up and saw that Eamon had returned, again gesturing for her to come along. *Nuts*, she thought.

EZWriter: I have to go. Thomas can we talk later? I have to get my report sent back to America.

SubDude99: Hold the phone! You're not in America? Where are you?

EZWriter: Ireland (grinning)....why, where are you?

SubDude99: London. Hey! I've got an idea....

EZWriter: London!...Sorry, Thomas, gotta run. Later.

SubDude99: Wait! You didn't tell me what you look like!

The next message on the screen flashed back, "EZWriter has signed off."

She was gone. He was intrigued. And for her part, she was curious and didn't want to leave, but she needed to be cautious, reluctant to give away too much information. And...Eamon was waiting.

chapter 4

TAKING CARE OF BUSINESS

> *Had I the heavens' embroidered cloths,*
> *Enwrought with golden and silver light,*
> *The blue and the dim and the dark cloths*
> *Of night and light and the half-light,*
> *I would spread the cloths under your feet:*
> *But I, being poor, have only my dreams;*
> *I have spread my dreams under your feet;*
> *Tread softly because you tread on my dreams.*

William Butler Yeats, 1865 — 1939 (Dublin)

Belfast

People generally took to Eamon Loftus instantly, with his altar-boy good looks, his clear tenor voice cultivated by years in the church choir, and his quick charming "crack" with friends in the pub. His talkative, friendly manner always won him a long draw of stout and a song accompanied by fiddle and bodhran drum. People often remarked that he would make a fine politician, and that might have been true if Eamon didn't hate politics so much. A quick thinker, drawing conclusions astutely, he was also quick to judge, like his father sometimes to a fault.

Wise old eyes, surrounded by a youthful face, hinted at Eamon's worldliness, developed from an accumulation of experiences with politics and close calls with violence from the time he was a small child. His acute sense of self and his mature decisiveness, however, hadn't stifled the boyish mischief in his personality, and the paradoxical character was a huge part of Eamon's charm.

He'd grown up in Portadown, a few miles southwest of Belfast. His widowed Protestant father had raised him, his brother, and two sisters with firm, clear values. Everything had been either black or white in the house of Michael Loftus. There had never been grey areas during dinner discussions. His father was an RUC officer — a fact that Eamon avoided sharing with acquaintances — and Michael could easily, in his mind, "separate the good guys from the bad."

Over the years Eamon, independent and experienced in political machinations beyond his father's imagination, quietly developed his own perspective, keenly aware of the "greys" in society, the issues that didn't have just one answer. Assignments which sometimes gave him the dubious luck to videotape terroristic incidents placed him on the edge of heart-wrenching situations. He had been on a peaceful assignment one night near Queens University and had unexpectedly caught on video the aftermath of an incendiary bombing in a pub two blocks from the University. Instead of total abhorrence, he empathized with both the victims' families and the bombers, whose cause he understood but couldn't fully embrace.

Close to graduating at the top of his political science

class at Queens University in the late nineteen-eighties, early in the spring Eamon was recruited by the Ulster Government to work as a "liaison". They told him he'd be assigned to attend rallies and report to his contact about suspicious activity that might be related to IRA maneuverings. He was not to point a finger but rather fill in the details of scant dossiers of individuals who showed indications of participation in the IRA movement.

At first he had no difficulty working for the government. For a few months he nosed around Belfast, posing as a videographer and using his boyhood hobby as a cover. But Eamon's nature was contradictory to the job, and very quickly his taste for what he was doing soured. At the same time, his love of videography blossomed. He'd been offered small jobs here and there and soon was offered a full-time position with a Belfast production company. Abandoning his political science studies and his father's dreams, Eamon immersed himself in his new trade and discovered, for the first time, a genuine joy in his work.

It was a contract between his employer and Maggie's that connected the American woman and the Ulster chap. His studio received a call from Toulouse in November asking specifically for a "talented and apolitical" videographer who could be loaned to the production company to travel with Maggie and film the people and locations in both Northern Ireland and the Republic while she researched and wrote her story. Eamon was eager for the opportunity to get out of Belfast and couldn't pass up an opportunity to travel with an American. He'd always been fascinated by their quirky Yankees ways and their entrepreneurship.

An avid romantic, Eamon was crazy about Maggie immediately, infatuated by her pretty face, her Midwest accent, and her American ideosyncracies. She seemed to enjoy his company but maintained an aloof, businesslike distance, oblivious to his adoration and his attempts to impress her with his brilliance and his wit.

He couldn't know that her bitter ending of a long relationship with Joe, a dominating control freak, had left her exhausted and craving time alone to re-establish her self-identity. He wouldn't have understood just yet that she'd had enough of men controlling her life, as far back as she could remember, and that much of it was too painful to recall. It was a perplexing role reversal that he, who could have the affection of any girl he wanted from the time he turned fifteen, would realize that she wasn't receptive to his unabashed interest in her. And although Eamon was sensitive and keenly aware of other people's pain, her diffidence bewildered him.

After working with her only three days, Eamon had fallen hard. He wanted to protect her, to make her laugh, dance with her, kiss her, take care of her. He'd do just about anything for her, and he had no clue of the opportunity he'd have to prove it.

* * * * * *

London

Thomas left the Tower Hotel for his morning constitutional across the Tower Bridge. He had a breakfast appointment with John Walker in the dining room of the hotel, and he wanted to take a brisk hike beforehand while he thought again about the information Philip had given him. He opened his umbrella, sheltering himself from the light morning rain, and focused on his impending meeting.

But phrases from his conversations with EZWriter kept interrupting his thoughts. *Tobler chocolate oranges... produce documentaries ... get my report sent back to America. Damn, I wonder where she is in Ireland and how can I meet her? ...missing me beauty rest, lad.* Ho, Ireland...next on his itinerary. He'd find out next time they talked, and he wouldn't let her disappear so quickly. He wanted to lift her veil of anonymity, know her more deeply than these brief online encounters allowed.

Inside the dining room, Thomas was seated at a booth in front of the windows overlooking the square. Throngs of people moved in unison along the sidewalk on their way to jobs. He surveyed the dark, wide wood, the brass finishes, the understated elegance of the fine old furnishings. While he waited for Walker, he thumbed through the Times, sipped coffee, and devoured a stack of wheat toast.

A tall man, well dressed, approached Thomas. He looked up and for an instant thought this might be Walker, but the man had no briefcase. Thomas was becoming impatient.

"Hello there, old chap. If you're done with the newspaper, mind if I take a look at it?"

Disappointed, Thomas replied, "Sure, help yourself."

"Thanks. American?" he asked, staring at Thomas. Thomas nodded and started to feel annoyed.

"Enjoying our city, seeing the sights?"

"Yes, thanks." Thomas deliberately looked at his watch and then out the window, as if to dismiss the stranger.

"Well then, have a good day." The stranger folded the paper and walked away. Thomas glanced toward a high-backed booth where the stranger sat down across from another person who was obstructed from Thomas' view. He shifted his chair around and glimpsed a redheaded man who looked like a dockworker, shabbily dressed and unshaven. *Now there's an unlikely pair,* he thought. Why the encounter made him uncomfortable, he had no idea, but he had an uneasy idea he was being observed. He turned his chair to face the booth directly...maybe this would discourage them from watching him.

He stood when he noticed the maître d' leading a fifty-ish, thin-haired gentleman in a trench coat toward his table. This must be Walker.

"John Walker? Hello, I'm Thomas deFremond. Would you like coffee?" He held his hand out to shake Walker's.

"Tea, thanks."

Walker removed his coat and sat down. "deFremond! Very pleased to meet you. I trust you're taking in some sights between business?"

"Yes, thanks. Saw a play last night. Pamela in your office got me a ticket. My first English play live in London, at the Globe...what an experience!"

Anxious to get on with business and avoid questions about his plans for the next few days, Thomas shifted in his seat and got down to business.

"I got some idea of your proposal from Philip Knight the other day. Can you tell me what you have in mind? "

Walker understood purposeful, no-nonsense business associates.

"Very well then. I've been with the firm since it started with mainframes and eventually moved into the PC market. Now the buzz is about linking and connectivity. We're heavily into videoconferencing and high speed printers. Color printers are making quite a stand in the home market. Are you a principal?"

"Not as a developer," Thomas answered. He'd watched Walker carefully as he talked, sizing him up. "The New York branch called me in as a consultant when they were dealing with imports, and now I'm in product development. We've acquired another company with three outlets that deal exclusively with corporate accounts, bringing the total to six. They specialize in local area networks and connectivity. I deal with specialty high-end items like computer aided design and videoconferencing. And I advise on new products. Many of the technical sales people come through me first. You have your own outlets?"

Thomas realized that John hadn't been briefed on who he was but simply that he worked for the New York office. That might give him the upper hand, and he wasn't about to relinquish it. Yet there was something inscrutable about Walker, something about his demeanor that made Thomas wary.

"Yes," Walker replied. "We need our own label. I usually work with some people who've been trying to market their own ideas but aren't savvy about how to do it. I think we could set up the English equivalent of your stores. But we need to do it right...start big to eliminate the competition. I envision a huge store like an American supermarket, with handcarts and checkout lanes. We can have the computers on the shelves. Blue light specials, with bells and whistles. We'll move a ton of them this way. We'll be the first."

Thomas feigned interest, nodding as he made mental notes. Encouraged, Walker continued.

"A chap near where I live has an injection molding company. He can make all the casings for our computers...he can make the cases for anything; battery backup units, our own desk clocks, printer stands, cables. We can package our own...get them made in Pakistan...package them with our own label. We'll get all the components from China, India or wherever, assemble them in the back room and eliminate the transportation costs. We don't even need to box the units, except maybe for mail order business. We can even ship them to the States if we go that route. We have so many engineers here, you wouldn't believe the labor force we can put together to assemble them. We're already doing that in my outlets...building our own machines."

"What about major brand names?" Thomas asked.

"We move them too. But the profit is in our own label."

"John, how are you suggesting we support the products if the customer just dumps them into a shopping cart and checks out at the cashier?"

"Service contracts like your Sears. But listen here, deFremond, let me change subjects for a moment. There's something else that I want to talk with you about." Walker leaned forward, looking at Thomas intently. "I see you know a lot more than Philip about computers. We have a contact who's looking to help his friend market a flat screen device he invented, but Mr. Holmes isn't convinced it's worth pursuing. However, I do."

Thomas didn't want to appear overly interested, but this was what he had been waiting to hear about.

"I don't know, Walker, I've already met with one company here that's attempting to market a flat screen for the CAD market. It's not all that impressive. Big, clunky and very expensive."

"No, no," John shook his head, "Look here,Thomas. My contact runs a marvelous fishing resort in the backwoods of Ireland. It's somewhere outside Belturbet in County Cavan. This inventor is a professor in Dublin but lives in Belturbet when he's not teaching, and the two are good friends. Anyway, his invention may be something innovative. Perhaps you could meet with him while you're here. I put some notes together for you on what we talked about. I'll get in touch with my contact Paddy, the fishing guide, and have him set up a meeting with the professor. What do you say?"

Thomas rubbed his chin, thinking about his next response, pretending to absorb this information as if it were all new to him.

"Well, I suppose I could make some time to look into it. I'll be reporting back to New York and will outline your marketing proposals to them. Philip's not really interested in hardware other than as marketable, movable products, but I'll take a look. Have this Paddy get in touch, will you? I could probably take a few days to visit Ireland."

"Thank you, deFremond. His name is Ian Pennton...Dr. Ian Pennton. I believe he's a professor at Trinity...not sure whether you'll find him in Cavan or Dublin. I'd prefer we keep this just between us for the moment, understand?"

"Yeah, sure."

"And will you have time to visit one of my stores while you're here? I'd really like you to see my operation."

"Sure, I could do that today. I'll make a few phone calls and come out to your office...say around one o'clock?"

"Right then. And meanwhile I'll arrange the meeting in Ireland."

The two men stood and shook hands. Thomas sat back down and finished his coffee as he watched John leave. He glanced around the room, noticing how busy the dining room had become during his discussion with John. The two men in the booth had gone.

Eavesdropping was inevitable in the close proximity of tables, and Thomas detected American accents among the diners. When their talk turned to technology, he couldn't help listening to the foursome at the table closest to his booth.

"I just got a computer. My kid has it all figured out already. It has a 32-speed CD-ROM reader/writer, a midi card, zip drive, the works, and I got an eighteen inch hi res monitor. It comes with all sorts of games, encyclopedia, and voice-recognition."

"Mine came with a sound card and huge speakers. My son is already putting together his shopping list of add-ons. He's downloaded all sorts of stuff off the 'net. He's on the thing from the time he gets out of school till I drag him off at betime. Next he'll want a mainframe for the basement. All he talks about is hookups and links and Bill Gates. Can somebody tell me what he's talking about?"

"My wife looked up the history of some rare disease that matched my father-in-law's symptoms and sent it to his doctors. This website has resources from the best hospitals in the country. You'd be amazed what you can find on that damned thing. The Internet is where it's happening."

"Did you read the front page of the business section this morning? They just discovered a new memory magnetic body at the molecular level. It's supposed to revolutionize computers...again. They say it'll be able to squash more information on a chip the size of a pinhead than a main frame can hold."

* * * * * *

When he returned to his room late that afternoon, Thomas contacted Philip to report on his meeting with John. He thought for a few minutes about his next steps. He didn't have much interest in the computer superstore idea — it was being done already — but the invention intrigued him. If there was anything to this professor and his invention, Thomas had no intention of including the British division in the game. In the first place, he liked the idea of contributing in some way to the development of Ireland's economic growth. But secondly, he suspected that if this Republic-based inventor found out he was working for a firm that was connected with a British corporation, Thomas probably wouldn't make much headway in sealing a deal.

He sent Matt a brief note and checked his email. Scrolling down the list of business correspondence, junk mail, and friends, he searched for EZWriter but found nothing. He opened a new email file and started writing. It wasn't easy...what do you say in a letter to a woman who's aroused your curiosity, yet you know so little about her? And he couldn't help wondering what she looked like.

TO: EZWriter

FROM: SubDude99

SUBJECT: (none)

Maggie,
   On my way to Ireland for a business meeting. Will be in Dublin, then County Cavan for a few days. Are you in the neighborhood? What are my chances of a rendezvous with a (fill in the blanks here, please) ___ feet ___ inches, beautiful ____ -haired, ____-eyed, _____- pound fellow American?
   Your faithful servant...Thomas

P.S. On the topic of fashion, what do you wear to bed? Tell me this and more about those chocolate orange things you mentioned when we met, and I'll tell you my most private dreams.

* * * * * *

In all things but love Thomas considered himself a cool cucumber...level-headed, self-assured, decisive. He knew what he wanted and he usually found a way to get it. That's what made him a successful scout, an invaluable asset to Holmes West. It was in matters of the heart, however, that Thomas floundered. The Mars and Venus thing, he assumed.

As soon as he thought he understood women, his lady of the moment would do something unexpected and women in general would once again prove to be the enigmatic sex. When he met an interesting woman, after a few dates he couldn't be sure she was really right for him. Or she just plain told him he wasn't right for her. Or she told him they were right for each other and scared him away. He was beginning to feel he'd never master his own romantic nature. And it was this uncertainty of his that drew women to him, another thing that perplexed him.

Hours later, Thomas hadn't stopped thinking about her. She wasn't just a curiosity, she was smart and witty, and he wanted to know her. Maybe if she knew him first? He would write another letter to her, this time dropping the flirtatious screen he typically used with strangers. He would tell her about his work, his interests, his life, his values, and he would ask her about hers. He truly wanted to know her, and this revelation startled him, for Thomas hadn't really wanted to intimately know anybody for quite some time. As he imagined her sitting beside him, sipping coffee, looking at each other (he hoped she had gorgeous eyes), the words began to flow.

* * * * * *

Hiking along the Antrim coast north of Belfast, Eamon proved his worth as guide, pointing out one site after another, leading Maggie to points of spectacular coastal views while checking out every angle for filming.

Sunshine washed over the water and landscape, chasing the chill from the winter air and gracing them with natural light for their work.

Starting at Lough Larne, they hiked and took pictures and video, and all the while Eamon entertained her with folklore about fairies and mythical gods, legends of Celtic rulers and heroic saints. Each stirring of leaves and crackling of twigs in the forest of Glenarm stoked her lively imagination with images of the "good people" hiding behind thick standings of trees and under the shimmering hoods of waterfalls.

Hitching rides along the road from willing motorists, they reached White Park Bay in mid-morning and began the ten-mile hike toward Giant's Causeway, the magnificent geologic wonder of thousands of geometric columns. Eamon kept Maggie amused by his seriousness as he discoursed with sincere reverence the story of the giant Finn MacCool, who, according to Irish legend, crafted the causeway as a crossing to Scotland.

Bushmills with its world-famed whiskey distillery

attracted Eamon's attention while Dunluce Castle's long romantic history beckoned Maggie. They resisted neither. The trek home was long and late in the afternoon. As the sun began its sudden, swift plunge to the horizon, the two travelers gave in to common sense and boarded a bus for Belfast.

"Thank God for these boots!" Maggie groaned as she sat down on the bench in the foyer of East Sheen and pulled her laces loose. "I'm exhausted." Eamon looked at her and swore to himself that she looked not weary but radiant. The flush in her cheeks and the sparkle in her eyes reflected her excitement at having discovered endless beauty everywhere they'd been.

"There now, darlin', let me help." Eamon bent over and tugged at her boots, then sat down on the foyer floor in front of her and began to massage her feet through her thick wool stockings. Her reflexes kicked in and she stiffened and tried to pull away. He was surprised by her reaction but held on firmly and deftly rubbed her arches and toes between his hands. Morgan bounded down the stairs and, at his master's command, plopped happily down on his belly and nuzzled his nose into Eamon's lap. Maggie began to relax.

"Better?" he asked, tipping his head and turning a crooked smile up at her.

"Aye," she smiled. She acknowledged him as more than a business associate, she was glad for his company. But she hadn't been touched by a man in a very long time, and certainly not with such tenderness. He possessed a compassion she hadn't observed in men before. He made her feel warm and comfortable. Her stiffness melted into a limp, tired slump. "Eamon," she put her hand on his shoulder and leaned down to give him a soft kiss on his cheek. "Thanks...today was...the best. Tomorrow, Cavan, right?"

Not waiting for a response she pulled her foot loose and leaped up, swung down to grab her boots, and hopped up the stairs. Before he could recover from the surprise of her sudden tenderness, she waved from the top of the steps and blew him an airy kiss goodnight. Then she was gone, and in a second he heard her door softly latch. He sat on the bench for some time, pondering the kiss, staring after her, until Reggie Williamson walked into the foyer and looked at him curiously, following his gaze up the staircase.

"She got you beat, lad?" Reggie asked, smiling wryly. "You're never going to understand them. Seems better to just push your heart back into your breast pocket and be on with it."

"Not me," Eamon said, "I've not heart for flakes like that one."

"Righto, me boy, I can see that now," Reggie quipped, winking at his wife. "You're in full control, and ye best keep it that way."

Eamon just kept looking at the empty stairway, eyes narrowed, brow furled. Women.

Up in her room, Maggie changed the roll of film in her camera, then lined up the camera, extra film, her notebook, pens, and map in a neat row on top of her dresser. Next, her backpack and boots were placed alongside the chair, positioned squarely parallel with the legs. Her jacket was hung in its place on the back of the vanity chair, her hat crooked over one shoulder. She'd never admit to being obsessive. Never mind Jane and George and everyone else who knew her well and teased her incessantly about her compulsive orderliness.

She turned to her computer, signed online, and read her email. A letter from Subdude99...Thomas? A meeting in Cavan? Oh, this was too close! She couldn't explain the tingle that went through her at the possibility of meeting him. She gasped at the "p.s." and then laughed. She was intrigued now, too, but still very cautious. Some inexplicable, subtle yearning tugged at her insides. Out loud, she whispered, "Uh-uh...I'm not ready for this." She wrote back to him.

TO: SubDude99

FROM: EZWriter

SUBJECT: re: (none)

Nice try, Thomas. I'll be traveling around and am on a schedule...so sorry, maybe another time. Send me your mug shot, and MAYBE I'll send mine. Wait a minute, take that back...I don't know much about you, and I'll be darned if I'll send my picture to a near total stranger. Give me some clues about yourself, and then I'll reconsider.

Fat chance! She thought to herself, then added,

p.s. In the winter, in Ireland, thanks to these ice-cold radiators...Cuddle Duds. Sleep tight, don't let the bedbugs bite...Maggie

She hit the "Send" button and belatedly remembered his question about Tobler oranges. She composed another letter to him.

TO: SubDude99

FROM: EZWriter

SUBJECT: Tobler orange...a gastronomically perfect experience

Thomas,
    One hasn't really lived until one has partaken of the fruit of the Tobler. Upon releasing it from its brightly colored box, one must carefully examine the "rind", an orange foil wrapped tightly around its "fruit", to find a labeled sticker. When this is removed, the foil can be peeled back. However, one must first perform the necessary whack on a hard surface with the label pointed down, slamming it hard and loud to detach the segments from the center rind.
    Now, Thomas, once this minor but noisily brutal act has been executed, one can relax and enjoy the task of undressing the fruit, systematically peeling the foil back, corner by corner, to reveal the equally split, perfectly shaped wedges. Before one's appetite has any chance to abate, the aroma of rich milk chocolate baptized with extract of orange wafts sensuously past the nostrils, which with their heightened sense will capture it and instantly beseech one's brain to deliver the command for further gratification.
    Seized by an irrational craving and delirious with desire for a taste of the fruit, one might then delicately pull one of the wedges free. Balancing it carefully between thumb and two fingers, one might bring the wedge up to awaiting lips quiver-

ing with anticipation. The pure delight of first contact between wedge and tongue can't be compared with any other pleasure in the universe. Drawn slowly into the mouth and alighting on ready, swollen taste buds, the flavor of the chocolate orange fetches such bliss that one must close one's eyes, abandoning consciousness of all else and letting nothing in one's surroundings interfere with complete and utter indulgence.

That, Thomas, is a Tobler chocolate orange.
Maggie

Once again she hit the "Send" button and sat back, smiling mischievously as she wondered how he would react. More and more she looked forward to his communiqués. As she pondered, her mail flag popped up, signaling the arrival of another letter. Opening the mailbox, she grinned as she spotted Thomas's screen name once again. Seeing his name on the list of incoming emails gave her a joyousness she didn't comprehend and didn't care to question. She decided to read it a little later, before she turned in. *It should make interesting bedtime reading material,* she mused.

Prolonging the anticipation of a bedtime reading, she re-checked her camera and equipment, laid out her clothes for the next day, changed into her thermals, quickly washed her face and brushed her teeth, then poured a cup of tea from the tray Violet had left outside her room a few minutes ago. With tea in hand, she snuggled under the covers and lifted her laptop over and onto the bed in front of her. A bite from a biscuit, another long sip, and she logged on to open the letter.

TO: EZWriter

FROM: SubDude99

SUBJECT: Dossier

> *My dearest Maggie,*

(oh, she liked the sound of that, and her eyebrows curved up in uncertain curiosity as she read on)...

> *I am writing this dossier — perhaps an exaggeration, since there's not all that much to expose — to convince you that I'm not just a one-dimensional name on a screen. Please bear with me. Talking about myself is something I don't do much.*
> *May I suggest that you add this letter to the notes I have already sent to provide you with an almost complete historical personal dossier...fingerprints and social security number available upon request (but only upon your request).*
> *I can't seem to figure out how to get others to write endorsements regarding my character to submit for your approval without explaining why or how I happen to be corresponding with a perfect stranger (at least, at this point, you seem very near perfect, but really you no longer are a stranger to me). I have met (note my frankness here) other women online and from those experiences believe I can anticipate some questions you might ask.*

He's the strange one, she supposed, and read on.

First, my ethnic origins. Born the last (and I believe unexpected) son of a litter of three. Brothers and parents are all deceased (a tragic accident, which I would have been part of if I hadn't acted like a louse and ducked out of a family trip). Father of Yankee stock, French ancestry, and mother of Anglican Scottish descent. Natural desire to build New England stone walls, to clear fields for planting, and a penchant for good Scotch are probably my most notable genetic traits (along with remarkable good looks and oft misunderstood sense of humor).

I listen to all kinds of music and have an extensive collection of old records, which I bought cheaply at used bookstores over the years. I've just acquired a new sound system because I love pure sounds without distortions. I played the clarinet in the marching band of my very expensive, very private high school.

I read a lot and visit bookstores frequently. My preference in books is catholic...not as in Catholic but as in universal as I tend to like almost any book I pick up. From Carl Sagan to mysteries. And lots of technical journals and books (generally work related).

I am not of any religious bent, by the way, having studied several of the major ones and not found a need for any one in particular. As a huge sweeping statement... I don't think if there is a God He has had much interest in Earth after He created it; otherwise, would He have left it in the care of humans? Possibly He has about as much interest in ants as in me...made 'em... they seem to work... move on to the next big project...like creating another galaxy somewhere else. Why hang around here when there are much more interesting projects out there? Billions and billions of systems out there. Is ours special? I sort of doubt it.

I've never been married. I have no offspring. One long-lived relationship. Over and complete, no loose ends, full closure.

I have no pets and I don't think about horses at all, although I went horseback riding years ago with a girlfriend whose brother was a TV cowboy character (does that count?). By the way, she wasn't a cowgirl but rather a nightclub exotic dancer and my landlady during my rebellious of-age phase. Perhaps you might delay asking me about that one until one day when we know each other MUCH better.

Considering all aspects of my personality I don't think I have any repulsive habits. (I am sure someone would have told me, since previous relationships have been very open to discussion). I am direct and will talk about any topic without restraint or restriction.

Personal hygiene is of normal concern. I have no unusual body odors, except when I eat a diet of nothing but garlic for a week or two (not terribly often, I promise...the garlic diet has been sort of an experiment — more on that later under the subtitle "healthy living"...or maybe not).

Healthy living: I'm not neat, not even close. My place is in a perpetual state of mess and I like it that way. But whatever neatness I lack in domicile and office, I make up for in mind and body.

My dreams are pretty much the same as everyone else's...sharing my life with my kindred spirit. (Kalhil Gibran is a good source here). As of late, Maggie, my dreams have seemed to always include you. Out of eight million or so people in this crazy world buzzing around the Internet, we found each other (gets into mysticism but let me continue anyway). We hit it off immediately. We like to talk to each other, and although I sense you are hesitant to get involved I think that you are equally mystified by me as I am by you. We should talk for a long time instead of these brief encounters! I admit you're driving me nuts!

You, Maggie, are a primary character in a frequently recurring dream, and I want to tell you about it. Okay (taking a deep breath), here goes...

Before I describe it to you, though, please understand that I don't usually think much about my dreams. However, this dream seems to be directing me down an avenue that I'm compelled to explore (more mysticism...but I can accept a certain amount of stuff I can't deal with). In advance, Maggie, I plead male mentality and beg your tolerance. I don't mean to offend, but I have to get this off my chest.

We meet and are somehow instantly in a bedroom, dancing to slow music in front of a crackling fire...(my dreams rarely include all the necessary connections of how to get from point A to point B). We also seem to be intensely physically drawn to each other, which is a mutual surprise to both of us and the surprise is expressed through our eyes and body language... uncontrollable twitches, trembles, comfortable unexplainable stuff that sets us both smiling and filling each other with new redirected thoughts of lust. In my dream, which seems to skip around, we find ourselves naked and in bed.

I should interject that the Internet has a wondrous way of allowing people to bypass many of the usual social tests in meeting someone. So does this dream. After only a few conversations with you and having already spilled my guts, I am not afraid to reveal my innermost thoughts...(a curious feeling of knowing you already...if I am mistaken...hmmm...ok...not sure how to handle rejection, but realize that you may decide that rejection is your next step, which I hadn't considered until now).

We've made love (my dream is far more detailed than I'll go into here) and now are continuing to explore each other. We're completely relaxed, satisfied and obviously intensely happy. We talk as we touch. I don't remember the words, just the feeling of being happy that we are talking and laughing. I remember now talking about nipples...that is, how we both have them and how yours are far more interesting. Sorry...I really don't mean to embarrass you.

At any rate, some of my other dreams tend to lean more to everyday living kind of stuff — reading, walking, eating ice cream together, cleaning house, shopping for groceries. So you can see why this one stands out.

I hope this letter finds you rested and content and of an open mind, and I wish I were there with you instead of here alone. Maggie, you make me

*feel comfortable and exhilarated, and I want to
know you completely.*
    Thomas

* * * * * *

Blushing, and a little but not too put off, repeating
phrases from his email in her mind, she saved his letter
and logged off. She settled back against the pillows, trying
hard to put a face to these phrases and musings. Damn, he
didn't even describe himself! She thought harder. Nothing
materialized, no defined image. It didn't matter. The flush
of embarrassment she felt while reading about his dream
dissipated with the recollection of the earlier parts of his
letter...his openness, his revelations about his spirituality,
his unpretentious way of "talking" to her.

    She wondered about his family and wanted to know
more about how they died. She made a note to ask him
sometime when she felt certain it was something he could
talk about. He trusted her enough to tell her exactly what
he was thinking, so did she owe him a reciprocal self-
analysis? Maybe, but if neatness was an issue, perhaps she
should sidetrack that subject for now.

* * * * * *

An hour later Maggie yawned and looked at the clock.
She had written back to Thomas, as openly, she hoped, as
he had written to her. She told him about Jane and Charlie,
her mother, her other brothers and sisters. She told him

about how religion had influenced her early life. She talked about wanting, as a child, to become a nun and how teaching had replaced that dream and fulfilled her until the urge rose to test herself in a career outside the confines of classroom walls.

She carefully avoided the blackest part of her life, not because she didn't trust him...no, for reasons she couldn't fathom she did trust him. But she wasn't ready to give that much of herself to him, to reveal the history of childhood abuse to which she and Jane had been subjected.

For now Maggie withheld, too, the truth that similar dreams had filled her nights lately, impassioned dreams in which Thomas played the ardent male lead and Maggie the responsive leading lady. No coy, cryptic messages were contained within her letter...it was direct and honest and carried with it the message that a covenant of friendship had been offered and securely sealed.

chapter 5

SHIPS PASSING — *MAGGIE* AND *EAMON*

Some say that the world is a vale of tears, I say it is a place of soul making.

John Keats

Maggie reached down from the side door of the old Eireann bus bound for the Republic while Eamon handed up their equipment and bags. They clambered to the back of the bus and got comfortable. There was not the usual crowd of people taking the afternoon leg to Cavan and destinations beyond, so Maggie lined up their bags in the back seats and plopped down on one side across from Eamon, stretching her legs over the seats. She hoped that his bad mood arose from having to leave his four-legged companion Morgan behind with the Williamsons and not for some other reason having to do with her.

Eamon's day had begun poorly. Besides fretting over having to leave Morgan behind, he was extremely irritated with Maggie. He looked sideways at her, scowled, and stared out his window. Exasperated, he turned back toward her and glared until she could avoid the confrontation no longer and looked back at him.

"What?" she snapped.

"You told this bloke your name??"

"Just my first name. He's not a bloke! Come on, Eamon, it's no big deal. He's nice. I like him."

"Are you daft? How can you like someone you've never met...Mags, darlin', you worry me. This online chatter could be dangerous. What do you know about this Thomas guy?"

"Chat, Eamon, chat...not chatter. Honestly, Eamon, this is the last time I tell you anything...you're just like my sister, only worse." She was avoiding his question and he knew it, but how could she explain to him a kind of relationship that was yet incomprehensible to her?

"Except she's not here and I am, and I'll look after you, my wee pet." He spoke earnestly.

Damn, he had a way of pacifying her, the devil! Tenderly, she laid her hand over his and smiled entreatingly. "I know, Eamon...just trust my judgment, alright?"

He didn't, and he wouldn't, and he simply gazed at her silently with smitten heart, barely concealed, then turned to look unseeingly out the window as the bus pulled out of the Belfast terminal and headed southwest toward County Cavan.

Two hours later they unloaded their gear at the bus depot in Cavan Town just as the evening dusk had turned everything a soft gray, then quickly deepened the skies to a liquid blue. The pair of travelers ordered a light meal while they waited for their car rental agent to pick them up. Out came Maggie's notebook and pen from her backpack. She began writing, her face reflecting her thoughts as she scribbled, an image that had become familiar and pleasant to Eamon. Later she would send installments to George and an email to Jane.

A little food and the assurance that Maggie was willing to do the driving improved Eamon's disposition to the point where the two were back on amiable terms. By early evening they had discussed their plans for the next few days.

Maggie watched Eamon as he rearranged their gear in the back of the tiny Golf and then unloaded their overnight backpacks at the hostel. "I'll bet when you were taking those political science exams at Queens, you weren't expecting that your next job would include hauling an old lady around the countryside chasing after castles and sheep, huh?"

"Oh, it isn't like that at all, Maggie." He smiled. "You have a way with words, and I have a way with a camera...we make a good team. Just give us Ulsters a break and don't make us all look like bloodthirsty terrorists...we have hearts and homes and families, too, you know. People just have the wrong idea about Northern Ireland entirely."

"Hey, I'm an unbiased journalist. I'll be fair. We'll make sure that people see Ulsters in a realistic light."

"Read me your notes from today, will you? Show me how you turn observations into words that make people think they were here, too, and I'll show you how I take a picture and make it look like you're standing right in it."

* * * * * *

To: LazyJane

FROM: EZWriter

SUBJECT: Heading south...

Dear Jane,
We've arrived in Cavan to begin our journey around the Republic. Eamon had to do some digging but he finally found a car rental place and got us a little car (emphasis on little, but just as well...these roads weren't designed for a Lincoln Continental). A Golf, I think it's called. The poor fellow was taken aback when Eamon pointed to me as the driver (Eamon hates to drive and says he's terrible, so I'm relieved he deferred to me), but he checked my license twice and then "passed" me after a short drive to check out my skills. Honestly, I think the "U.S." on my license countered the fact that I'm female, but he sure was reluctant to hand over the keys.

We turned right away toward Ballyconnell, a little hamlet Eamon suggested we should visit. Mind you, this was my first experience driving on the left side of the road in the pitch black of night, in a strange car with gearshift to my left, over barely two-lane, winding roads. Eamon hasn't yet collapsed from nerves, so we'll probably do all right in the daytime as well. We've decided to stay at a hostel outside of Ballyconnell. It's an old stone barn that sleeps about 35 people, with showers, a living room with fireplace, a big, fully equipped kitchen, and a gathering room. With the exception of a young man from Belfast who's occupying one of the thirty beds upstairs, we have the place to ourselves. I'm zonked out, ready for a

*long night's sleep warmed by the peat stove in my
room. Tomorrow morning I want to get a good
gander at this countryside surrounding us.*

Love, Magpie

*P.S. How's Mom? Give Charlie a big hug and
a slobbery kiss for me, will you?"*

* * * * * *

TO: goffing@toulouse.com

FROM: EZWriter

SUBJECT: Southern humor...

George,

*Attached is my latest journal. Am sending you
the videos and film today.*

*Now that we're out of Northern Ireland, I think
Eamon wouldn't chastise me so awfully for laughing at a little Irish political humor and wanting to
share it with you: Sean the IRA soldier is late to a
meeting at the Sinn Fein office. While zigzagging
down Falls Road, he comes upon Fr. Doyle trudging up the hill and, being a good Catholic, he
obligingly stops the car and offers Father a ride.
On their way again, Sean says, "Father, I apolo-
gize, but I'm late to a meeting and have to go
through Shankill, do you mind?" "Understand, my*

boy, 'tis fine," replies Father Doyle. Up in Shankill, Sean sees a Protestant minister standing outside his church and he instinctively swerves to hit him, but remembering Fr. Doyle, he turns the car away just in time and misses. Sean looks at Fr. and says, "Father, I almost hit that minister, sorry." "That's all right, my son," says Fr. Doyle, "I got him with my door."

Will have my next section for you in a day or two. Eamon's terrific...you won't believe the footage he's got.

    Maggie

* * * * * *

A chill washed over her face, and she nuzzled her nose under the cover, pulling the heavy quilt up over her face and drawing warmth from the rest of her body. Persistently, the chill air nudged her awake in the darkness, and she realized that the peat stove had burned out and the temperature in her room was dropping rapidly. A sliver of the rising sun over the hill beyond the pasture beamed through the dusty glaze of her window.

Yawning, she climbed out of bed, shivered and stretched, then slipped into her boots. She tossed more peat into the iron stove, grabbed her soap and towel, and jogged to the ladies lavatory. *Oh God, let there be warm water,* she begged. Braving the cold, she shed her thermals and jumped into the cold shower and screamed at the blast on her still-warm skin. Slowly the water heated up, and soon she didn't want to get out from under the warm stream.

Meanwhile, Eamon stood outside the hostel, drinking in the fresh, crisp air, the briskness of the morning, and watching the cows' breath curling around their heads. A devilish grin crossed his face as he snuck up on one of them. But when the benign beast turned to look at him with its big sad eyes, the city slicker backed off promptly.

"Mags!" he shouted, "Hurry up and get out here! You're missin' all the sunshine and dew!"

* * * * * *

Back in her room, dried and bundled into a thick wool sweater, jeans and heavy socks, she pulled her hair back and tied it carelessly. Then she opened her laptop and added to her journal.

Journal Entry — Ballyconnell, County Cavan
*   Hmmm...yup, if ya don't watch 'em, peat stoves burn out in the middle of the night and you freeze your buns off. We woke to yet another day of sunshine and soft Irish air, but this time out in the countryside, with cows grazing in the meadow nearby and the dew sparkling on the hills of the farm on which our hostel sits. This is country where the peat is "thick as toothpaste" according to our host, John.*

* * * * * *

She joined Eamon outside, exploring the barn and out-buildings, climbing the hill beyond to leisurely scan the countryside. Everywhere she looked, green pastures dotted with trees surrounded small farmyards and narrow lanes.

Breakfast finished, they loaded their gear and drove the few miles into Cavan Town. They found it something like Belfast, bustling with Christmas shoppers, but much smaller and more intimate, with narrow, winding market streets ridged with slush from a recent snow and a lovely town square where teenagers and housewives congregated.

Along a sloping side street a noisy flatbed truck ambled up the hill, followed by dozens of children filling the street and shouting, "Throw some to me!" She watched as the truck speaker blared out cheerful Christmas tunes and Santa Claus appeared, perched on a high chair in the back of the truck, waving, tossing candy to the children, and playing a pennywhistle accompanied by a musical "elf" band. A sign carried by more oversized elves and bringing up the rear indicated that this was the annual Christmas revue parading out of the children's theatre at the bottom of the hill.

In the afternoon they explored the county, passing through the village of Belturbet and meandering about the ruins of sixth century Drumlane Abbey with its round tower and spectacular view. While Eamon looked for unusual angles and views of the lake beyond the Abbey, framing it with the ancient stone passages and lookouts, Maggie read names and years on gravestones, wondering about the mysteries and stories harbored in the gray, lop-sided markers. Fascinated by churches despite her cynicism about religion, they stopped at the parish church in Milltown, paused in the small cemetery, then as dusk began to settle, drove up the gravel driveway of Stag Hall Bed and Breakfast.

The engine hadn't come to rest yet when the door of

the house opened and a strikingly beautiful woman with black hair and sparkling, dark eyes stepped out to greet them. Clad in a gold plaid wool cape, black leggings and black boots, Ceil Brennan smiled and held her arms out to Maggie, urging her to hurry into the warmth of the house.

"Ah, you've found us! You must be Maggie O'Connor and this would be Mr. Loftus? I'm Ceil Brennan. Come in from the cold and let's get you settled. I have some tea ready. It's frightfully cold this winter. We aren't used to having visitors this time of year, and you'll be having the place to yourselves mostly. Paddy," she called to her husband, "our guests are here. They have several bags, darlin'...oh, no, let Paddy get that for you!"

While her husband followed Eamon around to the back of the car, Ceil showed Maggie to her room, a well-appointed, luxuriously decorated room with blue paneled walls trimmed in white and gold, lit by tear-drop crystal wall lamps. A tray of tea had been set on a dainty dressing table.

Long experienced with American visitors who were generally unprepared for the damp chill of winter months in Ireland, Ceil had thoughtfully placed a modern heater and extension cord next to the radiator. Cold and weary, Maggie looked at the high, fluffy bed and thought fleetingly of the primitive barn and cots they'd slept in the night before. "Lovely," she sighed, looking at Ceil, who smiled back with satisfaction.

"Here's Paddy with your bags now. After you're settled, you and Mr. Loftus might like to join us in the parlor by the fire. I'll show Mr. Loftus to his room now." Quietly Ceil closed the door behind her, leaving behind the light, clearly feminine scent of her perfume wafting in the bedroom air.

Minutes later Maggie had downed a cup of tea, carefully surveyed the suite, organized her things in neat rows on the extra twin bed in the corner and lined up her toothpaste, brush, soap and shampoo along the window ledge in the bathroom. Satisfied that everything was in order, she had "set up camp" for the next few days and could now relax.

She sat on the bed, looking around the room, listening to the silence and feeling suddenly lonely. This is a room that should be shared by lovers, two sweethearts, she mused. Her thoughts turned to Thomas, and she began to imagine his face, his hands, his build, all completely a figment of her creative mind. She couldn't draw out the details of his face, but she pictured him walking toward her, sitting down on the edge of the bed next to her, embracing her, caressing her hair and murmuring comforting words to her. In her mind, he spoke deeply but softly, with kind words that lulled her into a security that had eluded her in past relationships. Phrases from his self-revealing letter drifted through her thoughts like a warm blanket, and she felt an attachment with this faceless person who had placed his trust in her. Could she reciprocate?

Sighing, she stood, stretched, and admonished herself. It's too soon to feel so much, she thought, be careful. Her experience with Joe had scared her. In the course of their affair, she had unwittingly surrendered her independence under his domination. Never again.

Yet, she missed the touch of masculine hands, a deep voice whispering intimate suggestions near her ear, blowing warm breaths on her neck. Maggie turned her head sideways, as if she was surprised by the sensation of his breath, then absent-mindedly brought her hand up to her neck, touched the concave of her clavicular notch and slowly slid her hand lower, over her left breast, tracing her fingers around in a tightening circular caress until the tip of her finger touched her aureole through her sweater and she felt the nipple swell and harden, her senses awakened. A deep ache filled her chest and soared down into her abdomen. She reached up to rub her eyes, and her mind came sharply back into focus on the present. *Never again,* she reiterated silently, *I won't just be an object of pleasure for some mean bastard.*

* * * * * *

Passing doors on the right and left, she found one labeled "Parlour" and opened the door to a large, low-ceilinged dining room and lounge with soft peach walls and a roaring fire, abundant Christmas decorations, and family photos. Ceil had set a tray of hot cocoa and biscuits on a short, heavy wooden table in front of the couch. Beside the hearth sat the two men in big overstuffed chairs, one with his back to her. Eamon looked up and beckoned her to the sofa, while her host, Paddy Brennan, reached for a match to light a cigarette. He turned and nodded to her, then leaned down and poked at the peat in the fireplace, sending up a stream of sparks.

A handsome man with thick gray hair and bushy eye-brows, Paddy Brennan embodied the Irish country gentle-man, comfortable in his role as host. The same height as Maggie, she thought he looked fit for his age, which she guessed to be about sixty-five or so. He looked much older than his wife, a black-haired, blue-eyed beauty who valued her appearance yet maintained a modest, almost self-effac-ing manner.

Paddy and Ceil had transformed the former Stag Hall Schoolhouse into a comfortable five-bedroom bed and breakfast. Set in the middle of lake-checkered County

Cavan, it had become a popular resort for well-to-do American and European businessmen who were drawn to the area for its rich fishing lakes and whose wives accompanied them for a week of spa treatments under Ceil's trained hands.

Never having ventured further than Belturbet, Paddy was a country gent who had captured the heart of a city girl and charmed her into sharing with him a quiet life far from culture-rich Dublin. They'd raised three restless daughters who shared their mother's desire for excitement and the arts and ventured to the big city to attend university, later returning to the country life their father so loved. Yet throughout their simple country life Ceil had never abandoned her own dreams of acting, dancing, and mingling with sophisticated folk.

Now, as Maggie sipped her cocoa, she strolled around the room, looking at pictures on the walls and tables. They were mostly family photographs, interspersed with pictures of Ceil at various ages, wearing a traditional Irish dance costume in one picture, riding a horse in another, standing with a group of people smiling at the camera. In the bottom corner of that photo, Maggie read, "Best wishes from one of the Playboys, Aidann Quinn."

"What's this picture of, this is you, right?" She asked Ceil when she came into the room.

Ceil brightened when she saw the photo Maggie was pointing at. "That," she smiled. "That's the time County Cavan became famous for a couple of days."

"Famous?"

"Aye, see that man in the center? That's Aidann Quinn. He filmed a movie here, called Playboys. A wonderful movie, it was, thought I don't suppose it got to America."

"Tell her why it was so wonderful, girl," Paddy chimed in.

Ceil blushed.

"She was an extra in that movie," he answered for her. "Just a split second on the big screen, you'll see her, but my bride made it into the picture shows, didn't ya, darlin'?"

"Aye, what a grand time that was," she said dreamily.

That evening, as Eamon and Maggie sipped their cocoa and listened to the peat fire crackling and Ceil's muffled, distant kitchen noises, Paddy regaled them with fishing tales and the history of County Cavan and its inhabitants.

There was Anthony, the rosy-cheeked corner store proprietor and county councilor, and Old Anthony, the decrepit, bent, gray-bearded senior who claimed to have fought in the First World War and thought each stranger to Belturbet might be an old army buddy. In a melodic lilt, Paddy described Father Carroll, the tall, thin, dry-witted priest of Stag Hall Parish, and several other residents of Cavan who preserved the history of Ireland's midland by living it daily.

The silky glow of the lamps, the warmth of the fire, and the lilt of Paddy's voice worked like a sedative on Maggie, and before long she leaned her head against the corner of the huge sofa and let her lids droop and her body drift into a contented doze.

* * * * * *

TO: goffing@toulouse.com

FROM: EZWriter

SUBJECT: Southern humor...

George,

Can you "bear" more Irish humor? Notice on an Irish building site: "The shovels haven't arrived, and until they do, you'll just have to lean on each other." and — Two Irishmen went to Canada for a hunting holiday. They decided to go to the Yukon to hunt. On the way, they saw a road sign that read, "bear left," so they abandoned the trip and went home.

Here's the next installment. I hope when you read it you get a good feel for the Irish hospitality we're experiencing. Thanks for wiring the expense money.

Maggie

* * * * * *

Wide awake and refreshed, energized by a shower and a pot of tea delivered by Ceil, Maggie used the quiet early morning hours to translate her notes into the next part of her documentary. After two productive hours, she joined Eamon for a full Irish breakfast. Then they packed a picnic lunch and set out for another day of exploration in County Cavan.

Ever the critic, Maggie was happily satisfied with what she'd seen of Eamon's photography so far. He had a knack for capturing on film odd tidbits of life that went otherwise unnoticed by lesser trained eyes. Both his wit and his artistry appealed to her creative, perfectionist nature, and she was glad for his companionship. They were both inclined to keep a flexible schedule, ready to ditch their itinerary if a more interesting option presented itself.

In the misty morning light they ventured through Killykeen Forest on rutted roads, over grassy hills and through moss covered woods to Lough Oughter, one of hundreds of lakes in County Cavan. Set deep in the woods, the lake was surrounded by bog oaks and unkempt hedges gone wild. Maggie ran ahead to the edge of the lake.

"Eamon, look out there, on the lake, a castle!" She pointed to a tall, narrow tower standing on a small outcropping of rock.

"A broken castle, that is," Eamon said when he caught up to her. "A bit run down, wouldn't you say? That'll never do when the kids and grandkids come along."

She frowned, then dismissed his teasing. "I wonder how we could get out there...look, I think it's on a little island!"

Eamon looked around and after a moment walked a few paces over to a big outgrowth. He pulled aside some weeds, revealing an overturned boat.

"I doubt the owner would mind if we borrow this."

Together they tipped it right side up, pushed it to the edge of the lake, and Eamon carefully stepped in. Assured that it wouldn't sink, Maggie climbed in and they rowed out to get a closer view of the remains of O'Reilley Castle, which was indeed perched somewhat precariously on a disproportionately tiny island.

"This was once a vast estate, can you believe it?" Eamon said. "The O'Reilley clan was an old family, and their land extended across several communities of tenants and small landowners. They were friendly landlords and protected their tenants as if they were part of the family. They literally ruled County Cavan for hundreds of years."

Maggie asked him then about King Rory O'Connor, and he described with surprising consistency the same stories of Celtic battles with the Norman invaders that her great-uncle had told her when she was a child.

Content to have Maggie to himself, Eamon relished the day. Joyfully getting used to losing their way, frequently they enlisted help from the locals by asking directions and were never disappointed. Just before noon they came upon a gent standing in the middle of the forest with his dog, silently gazing at the lake.

That's the Irish for you, thought Maggie — *contemplative, spiritual, taking time to appreciate the beauty enveloping them in its depth and its softness.*

Respecting the stillness, she shut off the engine and they sat quietly in the car a few yards behind the man, following his gaze and sharing the tranquility he'd discovered there. After awhile, he turned and smiled at them, then sauntered over to their car followed by his lagging dog.

"Lovely day, isn't it"?

After exchanging pleasantries, Maggie politely asked him for directions back to Belturbet. She grinned at Eamon when, typical of the country folk, the man's directions started with, "Well, it would be best if you didn't start from here..."

Winding their way through the forest, Eamon pointed to a fallen tree by a brook alongside the road.

"Pet, I beseech thee, stop thee hence and allow me to take sustenance before my body wilts before thee into pitiful nothingness."

"Good grief, Eamon," Maggie laughed, "Can't you just say 'stop here, I'm hungry'?

They parked, unloaded their basket of food, and got comfortable on a thick blanket of green grass near the fallen tree. Having satisfied their hunger with sandwiches and a thermos of tea that Ceil had stowed in a picnic basket for them, Maggie picked up Eamon's camera and started shooting photos in different directions while Eamon pulled a miniature book from his shirt pocket and began to page through it. He stopped halfway through, having found what he was looking for, a Percy French poem about a locale not far from where they sat. Skimming the words, and glancing at Maggie, he started reading aloud. Mesmerized by the words he recited in his clear melodious tone, she closed her eyes, allowing her thoughts to drift.

"The Garden of Eden has vanished, they say.
But I know the lie of it still.

Just turn to the left at the Bridge of Finea
And stop when halfway to Cootehill.

'Tis there you will find it, I'll go, sure enough,
When fortune has come to my call,

For the grass it grows around Ballyjamesduff,
And the blue sky is over it all.

And tones that are tender, and tones that are rough
Are whispering over the sea:

Come back, Paddy Reilly, to Ballyjamesduff,
Come home, Paddy Reilly, to me."

The lull of Eamon's recital and the hot tea drunk from the thermos made Maggie drowsy. She leaned back against the tree stump and pictured the valley around Ballyjamesduff. It was so easy to feel as if you'd been transported back in time, perhaps eight hundred years, when you looked around the countryside and saw little evidence of contemporary Europe. Eamon's lilting voice hypnotized her, and she dozed.

Her subconscious took over, playing out a fantasy in which she was alone on the edge of a meadow, climbing over a low stone wall. She floated over meandering, barely discernable paths through the velvety green forest, her feet hardly touching the mossy floor. Her hair was long, curling down near her knees, and her diaphanous gown trailed behind her as she lightly skipped along a path. Then, somewhere along the way, deeper in the woods, the shadow of a darkly clad masculine figure blended with the trees, slowly moving toward her.

Suddenly she was running away from the dark figure and he was gaining on her, and the thrill of anticipation, escaping and then almost being caught in his arms, made her laugh. She glanced backward, losing her breath, ready to call to him, when she saw him fly around a tree not twenty yards behind her... But now she saw that it wasn't him at all, it was an ugly man, a horrid man-beast, and he was getting close. So close that she could smell his putrid breath and his oily body, see his bulging, teary eyes glaring at her hungrily. Panic-stricken, she tripped on a tree root and fell. She cried out as he approached nearer. Her fantasy had changed to a nightmare, the old one that she couldn't bury.

Eamon studied her while she dreamed. Her eyes twitched now and then, and her body transformed from a relaxed slump into tense rigidity. Carefully moving closer so he wouldn't disturb her, he frowned, wondering, *What is she dreaming that's got her guts aflutter?* He watched as her soft, smooth hands gradually clenched into fists that turned the knuckles white. Softly he touched her fingers and drew back...they were cold as ice. Her brows furled in an anxious wrinkle, her mouth closed tightly in silent fear, and her shoulders hunched forward, as if she was protecting herself from something. He bent down and leaned close to her face, feeling her quick, hot breaths on his eyes.

A cool shadow covered her and a warm breath tickled her face. Startled, she jolted awake and her eyes flew open to see someone above her. At first she didn't recognize Eamon. He looked alarmed, firmly holding onto her trembling shoulders. She couldn't speak and stared at him wide-eyed, frightened and disoriented. He, too, was shocked and didn't know what to do.

Shaking, chilled, she cried silently, then sobbed, and Eamon held her gingerly while she clung to his arms and sobbed louder and louder, her body wracked with anguish, gasping between breaths. "Maggie, darlin', it's okay, it's okay, you're safe, you're safe."

Alone on the edge of the woods, the two huddled together while she cried her heart out, unable to speak. Horrified for her fears, whatever it was that tormented her, Eamon held her, stroking her hair and rocking her, afraid to make a wrong movement, praying for the ability to console her from whatever evil plagued her. She curled up into a ball, half cushioned by his chest and half perched on the log.

For fifteen minutes they sat tightly embraced on the log while Maggie cried. He wrapped her icy fingers in his, massaging warmth into them. He made soft, cooing sounds, like a mother does with her crying baby, and the vibration of the cooing from his throat hummed against the top of her head, transferring warmth and security.

Gradually a calm crept through her, and her cry slowed to a sniffle. Puffy-eyed and red-nosed, she looked at Eamon and shook her head and smiled miserably. Even her mouth felt bloated and bubbles formed as she tried to talk. But finally she spoke, and for the first time she said out loud the words of the story behind the demon that haunted her.

* * * * * *

At ten years old, Margaret Marie wasn't ready to allow anyone to replace her daddy. Despite the drinking and the beatings she sometimes saw her mother brave, for whatever unexplainable reason she idolized him. He was tall and smelled masculine, like Hamms beer, and hugged her often. But finally, her mother could take no more abuse, and the restraining order kept her father away from them from then on.

No, it certainly wasn't her choice for there to be a new man in the house, and she and her clan of brothers and sisters unwillingly followed their mother and her new husband out to the country and the little wooded acreage. The children loathed their step-father, resentful of the orders he barked at them and the spankings he administered when they failed to do their work the way he expected them to. They despised him for changing their mother and hated that his meanness took the sparkle from her beautiful eyes and the song from her melodic voice.

Their consolation was each other, and they made their own happiness in the countryside, riding horses, creating adventures in the woods, exploring hunting cabins by the marshy lake, burying themselves in books, hiding in hilly pastures far beyond sight of the house. Maggie and Jane played pranks on the boys in the house down the road and giggled at their own childish antics.

One sunny late September afternoon, just after her

eleventh birthday, Maggie walked through the horse pasture, heading for her private place in the woods and singing a Beatles song under her breath. He came up behind her and walked alongside her. They passed the horses and the chickens, and with her city-kid naiveté, Maggie asked him, "How are eggs made?"

He needed no more of an invitation. The man said, "Let me show you," and took her arm, leading her toward the shed. A silent alarm went off in her head, but he gripped her arm firmly, and she didn't understand. He was a grownup and grownups are always right, so she fearfully obeyed.

Poor Maggie. If only she had possessed the confidence to instead pose that question to her newfound friends, who had been born and raised on farms. The next few years, and indeed her entire life from that day forward, would have been so much kinder.

However, it was her opportunistic step-father to whom she asked about chickens and eggs and thus set a thorn-ridden path which Maggie and her brothers and sisters would traverse throughout their entire adolescence. Years passed, and she said nothing to anyone, not even after he showed her sister Jane how eggs were made, not even after her brother ran away from home.

Maggie left home the day after she graduated from high school. Eventually the man left their lives and anger overtook her fear and she finally talked once with a psychologist, but by then the damage was permanent and no amount of talking could undo the hurt. She buried the demons as deeply as she could, never forgetting but never allowing her past to rule her life. She'd survived, but she was deeply wounded. And wounds like that are slow to heal. The senseless and overwhelming guilt that accompanied the burden of degradation had formed a protective, impenetrable film around her soul.

To Maggie, it meant she could never be perfect, she would always be flawed. She didn't realize that everyone is flawed. Control became her armor, and with it precision and compulsion and obsession for neatness, and from then on most everything Maggie did was contingent on self-assurance that she could protect herself from more emotional and physical damage. Only rarely did she lay down her mental armor and let her sensitivity breathe fresh life into her.

* * * * * *

She looked up anxiously at Eamon, fearful of what she'd see in his eyes. Tenderly he comforted her, his own tears glistening, desiring only to blot the anguish from her heart, wanting to coat her soul with a soothing salve. She saw this in his gentle look, and she was grateful. Now he knew things about her that nobody other than Jane knew, and it was okay.

"Pretty crummy stuff, huh?" she sniffed and blew her nose again, looking away down the road beyond the car.

"Ach, darlin'...no child should have to carry such a burden. Twasn't your fault, you know!"

"I know, I know. Every once in awhile, Eamon, I have this dream where he's coming closer and closer, but then I look him straight in the eye and give him a fast, hard knee in the groin, and after he turns white and can't move, he just crumbles into a thousand pieces."

They stared off into different directions of space, trying to imagine the shattering of wickedness, and then, quite suddenly, Eamon reached over and pulled a tuft of her hair.

It was enough to startle Maggie right out of her thoughts, and she shot a defensive glare his way. Then she realized what he had done, and slowly she smiled again. Together they let all their opposing emotions flood through them, and overriding her sense of propriety, she screamed through the still spaces between the trees, and then they cried and laughed more, howling at the ugly misfortunes of childhood, hugging and rocking in each other's arms. Moments later they settled down and as they drew apart, Maggie put her hand on his and quietly said to him, smiling, "Eamon, Eamon...I think you just whacked the orange."

"Sorry?" His perplexed look made her laugh again, remembering the silly conversation online the night she met Thomas.

She shook her head and smiled. "Never mind....but thank you."

"C'mon, pet, time to find our way back. Let me get some water to wipe that darlin' mug of yours."

* * * * * *

Maggie's revelation and Eamon's sensitive response opened a door to her emotional cell. She felt ready to embrace a new freedom, a passage to inner serenity. She could feel herself beginning to move in that direction and knew she had taken a good first step. The next time she logged online, Thomas was waiting for her, and they talked for hours, friend to friend, serious now, then laughing, rushing to tumble the words out, their fingers racing over the keys, delighted and tingling with the deliciousness of opening up to each other.

When their conversation turned to a comparison of

their very different upbringings, Thomas accounted frankly the coldness of his wealthy childhood, the hollowness of his bland relationship with his father, and the rich encouragement his mother gave him to think for himself. She could sense his profound sorrow as he told her about losing his whole family in the airplane crash and how it took him years to get over the unreasonable guilt he felt for having bowed out of that fateful family trip, being left the sole surviving deFremond.

Surprised and empathetic, Maggie calmly described for Thomas what her poverty-ridden life had been like in the fifties and sixties...the government surplus food, the condescending looks of neighbors when her mother had to ask to use their phone because she couldn't afford the monthly service, and working in the school cafeteria to earn hot lunches because they had no money to pay for it. She told him then, suprising herself even as she was glad for the opportunity, about her twisted step-father, the unspeakable cruelty she and her sister endured, and the irrational guilt she, like Thomas, had felt over circumstances she couldn't control.

They talked about the happy parts of growing up, too — the pranks pulled on private school peers, the games siblings played on the large, sloping front lawn of the acreage, the rock band of sixteen-year-olds that secretly practiced in the garage when Thomas' father was away at work, skating races across the frozen lake in tag teams of brothers and sisters.

They compared their coming of age moments of independence, during which each resolved to claim and preserve sole control of their lives. Their mutual interest in learning more about their common Celtic heritage spurred discussion about Maggie's documentary.

Neither Maggie nor Thomas asked for nor wanted sympathy, so perhaps it was fortunate that neither of them could see or hear the tears for lost innocence that flowed at either end as they typed their responses back and forth, Maggie crying for Thomas' absence of family, Thomas crying for Maggie in repulsed comprehension that any human being could inflict such depravity upon a child. The emotions that wracked their souls had drained their energy, and at three in the morning both could hardly keep their sleepy eyes open. Yet they didn't want to part for the night, and it was with profound reluctance that Maggie finally signed off and fell into a sleep that was deep and free, for once, of nightmares.

* * * * * *

TO: LazyJane

FROM: EZWriter

SUBJECT: Past, Present, Future

Dear Jane,
*   I've had a revelation. What the monster did to us doesn't have to control us. I'm liberating myself from the past. Want so much to talk with you. Will call in a day or two.*
*   Love, Maggie*

chapter 6

SHIPS PASSING — THOMAS

Belturbet

Thomas and Dr. Pennton had been sitting at the front corner table in the pub talking for an hour and a half. Several empty pints sat on the table...both fancied themselves hardy men who could hold their stout well. Everything had been said, Thomas had told the professor why he was there and everything he knew. Ian Pennton, a gifted storyteller, had steered Thomas away from business and then back again, and Thomas had followed his lead, glad for the diversion.

Now they fell silent, each reflecting on what they had shared, one looking to the street, the other toward the dark interior of the pub. They had sized each other up and neither had any reason to dislike or mistrust the other. Silently Pennton scrutinized Thomas once more while he thought about their discussion. It wasn't often he felt a kindred trust in someone other than his wife Kathleen.

Thomas waited patiently, studying a long, crooked, crusty tear in the wallpaper behind the professor's head. A flash outside interrupted his thoughts, and he shifted his focus through the pub windows into the bright daylight where the sun danced on wet bricks, to a sign that swung in the breeze, reflecting the sunlight. His eyes sparkled with anticipation about a potential joint venture with this old man, and he looked far beyond the street, already sealing their partnership in his mind, strategizing their next steps together. Finally, the professor turned to Thomas, smiled and cleared his throat to speak.

"Thomas, my boy, you're a good man...I believe you've a good head on your shoulders. But what makes you think I'd ever want to work with an American firm that's connected with a British company? My homeland is the same as my heart...I've no interest whatever in filling the pockets of some cockeyed cockney across the water."

"Dr. Pennton, after what I've heard, I don't know why you'd want to work with Holmes Worldwide either. You probably don't need to. But if you'll let me call some people, I think Holmes West may have some independent American investors who'd help you patent the device as an Irish product and manufacture it here in Ireland."

"Sorry, I don't think so. Don't want anything to do with the Brits at all."

"Well then, we'll find a way to do it without Holmes. I want to work with you. We'll make it work any way you want."

Ian leaned toward Thomas, and looked him sharply in the eye. "You're the first person, Thomas, who's comprehended the impact that Device 879 could have on the industry. More importantly, on Ireland's economy. I'll thank Paddy for puttin' you on to me." He looked out the pub window at a woman sweeping the sidewalk in front of a florist shop across the way. "Ah, Rosie's closing shop for the day, time to be headin' home. Thomas! Join me...come meet my Kathleen and have supper with us!"

Thomas was surprised by the professor's energy as they hiked, at Pennton's insistence, the two and a half miles from the pub to his cottage, where Kathleen had dinner waiting. She spotted the pair approaching down the road and set out another place at the table. Ian looked to the window from twenty yards away and waved hello to her. Then he signaled a silent message, and she nodded. Ian took Thomas's elbow and turned, guiding him to the back yard.

"Just a moment, Thomas, come with me. I want to show you something before we go into the house."

They stepped through the heavy shed door into the lab. Thomas gazed around in awe until his eyes rested on the object the professor held in his hands. Ian trusted his instincts, which told him to place his confidence in Thomas; he saw in Thomas an ally, a good man, and he began to explain his invention to him in detail. What Ian and his new acquaintance didn't see was the shadow of someone who peered secretly through the small back window, then disappeared into the woods just a few steps beyond the shed.

* * * * * *

That evening, having walked back into Belturbet to pick up his car, Thomas drove into Cavan and checked in at the Cavan Arms, a hotel on the outskirts of town. He was excited about Dr. Pennton's device and was absorbed in formulating a plan to produce it. But thoughts of Maggie crept in again and again until he could concentrate on the invention no longer.

Before retiring, he had recalled with exhilarating clarity the details of their two-hour online conversation of the previous night. He re-read her letter completely, reflecting. What was going on here? She moved him...he dearly wanted to see her, touch her, know she was real.

He skimmed through the Internet routing detail that followed her letter at the bottom of the email. His eyes stopped on the name "Cavan" and he realized her message had originated from Cavan Town. Damn. In their whole conversation last night it hadn't occurred to him to press her for her whereabouts. Connecting with her online was an unexpected encounter, and for once their exchange had completely satisfied him for the moment. But now, knowing she was nearby, his desire to see her in person overwhelmed him.

TO: EZWriter

FROM: SubDude99

SUBJECT: Urgent

Maggie,
If you're still in Cavan, please call me. I'm staying at the Cavan Arms, phone number 499523979. Please reply soon, I want to see you.
Thomas. P.S. Am recollecting your account of Tobler orange experience and now have begun a hunt for said delicacy.

* * * * * *

TO: SubDude99

FROM: EZWriter

SUBJECT: re: Urgent

Thomas,
I'm not ready for this. Be patient with me,
please? Besides, I'm on my way south and am
being held captive to Eamon's schedule. He wants
to return to Belturbet for Christmas with our hosts
at Stag Hall. Heading south now. I'll write later,
my friend. Maggie

It pained her to write this. She really did want to meet
him, and she hated to play cat and mouse with him, but for
so many reasons, it wasn't right yet. She had a job to do.
She didn't know him well enough yet (or did she?). And
she was still carrying emotional baggage that she didn't
want to get in the way when she was finally ready. The
time would come, if he would only wait.

* * * * * *

The coincidence! The irony of it drove him up the
wall. Thomas sat in front of his laptop in his hotel room,
pounding on the keys and reading out loud as he wrote.
Nothing sounded right. All he knew was that suddenly the
desire to meet her was consuming him. Nonplussed, he

looked at his writing, raised his brows and swore. Exasperated with his sudden inability to express himself with diplomatic finesse, he held down the backspacing key to retract his words and started again for the seventh try.

TO: EZWriter

FROM: SubDude99

SUBJECT: from Cavan

Dear...Dearest Maggie...elusive woman...HEY YOU!
    Why didn't you tell me earlier you were here?
You didn't even hint that you were nearby, much less
right here in County Cavan! Okay, so you hinted.

No, too remonstrative....try again....

Dearest Maggie, to put it frankly, I HAVE to
meet you. I have to meet the woman who's filling
my nightly dreams. I am here and you are close.
Pick a place..anyplace...and I will find you. Your
faithful servant,
    Thomas

Thomas positioned his finger on the "Send" button, squeezed his eyes shut and depressed it. *Sounds desperate,* he thought, *now she'll never agree to meet me.* He sighed, paced across the room to look out the window, and pulled his bulky sweater over his head. Leaving the hotel, he looked up and down the street restlessly, turned left for a few paces, then swung around and ran back to his room to send another note.

TO: EZWriter

FROM: SubDude99

SUBJECT: p.s.

Dearest Maggie,
I would e-mail you a photo of me but removed it from my laptop for this trip. I had to take all unnecessary files off my hard drive to make room for software and business files. My picture was not one of those I would put into the category as essential to have with me and okay, maybe I'm not exactly a dashing prince (but daresay I have other resources available to sweep you off your feet). However, I trust you carry yours with you at all times. Please! Please send it to me immediately!!!
Thomas

Thomas sat back in his chair, watching the monitor. He logged online, clicked the "Send pending e-mail", and continued to stare at the screen, willing an immediate response, drumming his fingers, looking expectant, as if he sensed that Maggie would be on the other end waiting for him. Still he jumped at the computer's announcement, "You have mail." He tipped over his coffee. As quickly as his fumbling fingers would obey his brain, he flipped through the screens to get to the open mailbox.

TO: SubDude99

FROM: EZWriter

SUBJECT: re: p.s.

No way, bud! You first. ;-)

His mouth formed a silent *what?*. He gaped at the words, imploring an explanation. Which email was she answering? He checked the transmit time. They were online together...missing each other by seconds! Thomas searched for her name on his buddy list. *EZWriter* was in brackets...she had logged on and signed off before he noticed. He shook his head, laughed and buried his eyes in his hands. Then he thought *what the hell* and composed another e-mail, going for broke.

TO: EZWriter

FROM: SubDude99

SUBJECT: re: re: p.s.

Dearest Maggie,
    I just received your cryptic reply. It sounded explicit, yet I'm afraid I don't understand. I hope you meant that if I send you my photo — if I can get it to send to you — that you'll send me yours?

Let's forget photos for the moment. I'm here in Cavan, only minutes away from you at most. I'll meet you under any circumstances you name. I'm sure I'll recognize your voice instantly. Okay, so I have never heard your voice. But I'm pretty sure I can recognize a midwestern accent here, at least.

Time out. If you're thinking I'm nervous and that might explain my inane emails, I'd like to think you're right. But Maggie, I'm serious about this and about you. May I suggest that you pick a time and a public place where we can meet? We can meet! We should meet. Please meet me (I'm on my knees now imploring you, almost begging for an audience ...figuratively speaking as I can't conveniently reach the keys to my laptop if I really kneel down.) (music starts to play softly here) "Then if it don't work out....then if it don't work out....then you can tell me goodbye-bye." Remember that song? Great melody for slow-dancing. Waiting to hear from you, hoping you'll respond in the affirmative.

Thomas

He scratched his chin as he finished it, paced around the room once more and returned to the screen and hit the "Send" button.

It was fortunate that for the next two days the professor kept Thomas occupied reviewing the documentation on Device 879 and showing him shelves of other inventions. By the time he had sent his last email to her, Maggie had already logged off. She couldn't retrieve her email while exploring the backroads of the southern counties. Thomas received no reply from her.

* * * * * *

Whether the serenity of the Irish countryside played magic with Maggie's soul, or whether it was the "cleansing" she experienced by confiding her childhood pain to Eamon and Thomas, Maggie couldn't be sure. She knew only that she felt at peace and truly the most optimistic she had been in ages.

Never having had a strong faith in psychoanalysis, psychiatrists or psychologists — after all, she reasoned, they're only human too! — she couldn't imagine herself in years of therapy. Yet she knew she needed to unload the burden of the responsibility she'd assumed as a child, and talking about it with a friend, a good listener, was at least a start. Opening up to Eamon had been a giant departure from her usual reserve.

She recognized that the trauma of her childhood had greatly molded her into the adult she had become. But the prospect of delving deeply into it to discover how it shaped her morals and her self-perception was too frightening to her. Maggie feared even more, however, with a paranoia that was unusual for her, that a therapist would attempt to instill new values and beliefs in her that she didn't want to adopt. Basically, she thought, she liked herself and believed herself to be a fundamentally good person.

It was too complicated, this therapy stuff, and she didn't want to have to muck around with the past in order to move on with her future. Rationalizing, she supposed.

Steering her thoughts away to avoid dealing with the answers, Maggie now directed her attention to Eamon. She perceived Eamon differently than she had when she first met him. Critical of him at first, quietly disapproving of a boyishness that she judged to be self-centered and immature, she had quickly gotten used to his jovial ways and even behaved less reticent around him. Now she saw in him a dependable, compassionate man on whom she could lean without forfeiting her independence. She let down her guard, trusted him, and treasured his presence in her life.

Together they traveled south, exploring, visiting with farmers and shopkeepers, county workers and school teachers...shooting video and photos, journaling and documenting the ordinary, simple lives of the rural Irish. They zigzagged across the countryside, first to St. Columba's in Kells, then to Slane Castle. Were the Irish intent upon hiding these historic treasures, she asked Eamon, or was the lack of road signs an assumption that one would always find his way by the use of landmarks?

No, replied Eamon, the lack of signs was a way of coaxing the timid visitor to corners of the country they'd otherwise regretfully overlook. The rewards, admitted Maggie, were worth getting lost several times each day. Besides, she realized, she was becoming a master at backing up, turning around, and looking to the right before turning left. "Lefts are good, rights are bad," they chimed in unison, giggling like a pair of school kids on holiday as she would once again put the car in reverse.

Onward they forged, taking notes and listening with great interest to the historians at Millifont Abbey and Monasterboice. They roved the fields of the Battle of the Boyne. They explored the 5,000 year-old tomb of Newgrange where once each year at winter solstice, the guide told them, the sun pierces a laserbeam path to reach the inner depths of the tomb, an event witnessed by a select few people huddled inside, surrounded by Celtic carvings on the walls.

They toured Kilkenny Castle and continued south to

the Waterford Crystal factory, where Maggie interviewed glass artisans whose handiwork was admired the world over. The continual sound of glass crashing and splintering into hundreds of pieces puzzled them.

"Aye, that," their guide explained. "Our glassworkers break any piece with the slightest flaw rather than pass it on to seconds shops. There are no seconds at Waterford Crystal!"

Here she found a miniature mantel clock embedded in Waterford crystal for Jane and for herself, a tiny crystal camera that would always remind her of this time with Eamon.

A day later they found themselves in Wexford on the Celtic Sea, setting up base at a bed and breakfast playfully called the Bull Ring Inn. The pair was ready for a respite and the blarney of their host Timmy, a worker on the Wales ferry.

* * * * * *

TO: goffing@toulouse.com

FROM: EZWriter

SUBJECT: Heading south...

Last night we drove in pitch black, except for a sky full of bright stars and a sliver of moonlight, toward southern parts. The roads really are incredibly narrow with no shoulders but rather, banked by shrubs, stone walls, or high earthen mounds, so you "feel" the narrowness as well as see it.

Along the way, we were startled by the sudden appearance of a big white head floating into the road in front of the headlights...no doubt it occurred to Eamon, just as it did to me, that this might be one of those banshees we've been warned to avoid at night. Let me tell you I was relieved to discover that, right there at the edge of the road was a cow poking its head out from a feeding trough to get a better look at us!

* * * * * *

One evening, enervated by days of research, exploring, and interviewing people, reluctant to remove her fleece-lined jacket to face the chill of her room at the Bull Ring Inn, Maggie sniffled and cried silently. It wasn't explainable, this self-pity, she just plain needed a good cry. She was happy, content...or so she thought. At this moment, though, she was confused by her deepening affection for Eamon and questioned her strange liaison with a faceless man named Thomas. She wanted to stop feeling anything for just a little while. At the same time, she wanted someone to hold her, comfort her. Eamon was kind, funny, and brilliant in his work. Thomas stirred something in her, but was he "real"?

She hurriedly wiped the tears from her eyes and answered a soft knock on her door.

"I brought you some tea and biscuits, pet." Catching the remnants of tears and a shiver as she folded her knees up under her chin and wrapped her arms about them, Eamon set the tray down and sat next to her on her bed. "Ah, Mags, you're not used to our damp winters, are you? Let me warm you up...good, there now, better?"

Feeling foolish, she smiled and nodded, leaning into

his welcome warmth. He rocked her back and forth, patiently whistling a tune while she felt her bones warming up and her muscles relaxing.

"I could sleep like this, Eam," she murmured, looking up at him with heavy eyelids. He grinned and gave her a quick tight hug, then impulsively leaned down and kissed her lightly. She closed her eyes and stayed there, didn't pull away, and kissed him back. They shifted together into a closer embrace and kissed again, slowly, deeply, then to her surprise, he gently eased her away from him and turned her around to face away from him. He wrapped his arms around her again, pulled her back against his chest, and gave her a light squeeze.

"Mags, pet...no." He shouldn't need to say anything...she knew better than he that this wasn't right for them, not right now, as much as he wanted it. But she twisted around to look at him questioningly, and she didn't understand the sadness in his eyes. He was feeling a wisdom that most people only gain in their senior years, when it's too late to have made the decisions that they wish they had when they were younger.

He closed his eyes, wanting to push aside his better judgment. But he knew already what it would take her only a little more time to recognize...something else was driving the passion in her at this moment. He didn't want to be associated in any way with the terrible memories of her childhood. Intuitively, he knew that taking her now would be just that...taking her. Instead, he wanted to help her heal first, help her understand that sex wasn't just a function of satisfying a man. When she came to him, there must be nothing steering her except a desire to be with him. He wanted to teach her the joy of making love. *Leave the door open,* he thought...*make her take time, but leave the door open for her.*

"Friends," he whispered, not as a question but with finality, so she couldn't protest...so she wouldn't hear his regret in wisdom winning over impulse.

* * * * * *

A long, restful night of deep slumber re-energized her. She awoke with a luxurious stretch and yawn, slid out from under the heavy blankets and reached up to lift the curtain aside a sliver. Sunlight streamed over her, and she leaned back for another lazy stretch. Lying on her back, she opened her eyes and focused on the ceiling, then let the focus blur as she tried in vain to picture Thomas on the white canvas above her. She must have dreamed about him, because he was on her mind when she rose out of semi-consciousness. Smiling with the recollection of their last encounter, she wondered if he'd written again.

She jumped out of bed, pulled a flannel shirt out of the closet and put it on. Then, in another compulsive motion, she lined up the hangers in the wardrobe exactly one and a half inches apart. Satisfied, she tugged her heavy wool sweater over her shirt and carried her laptop over to the bed. Tracing the cord of the telephone around the corner just outside her bedroom door, she plugged it into her computer. While she waited for the system to launch, she brushed her teeth, drew the curtains wider apart to let sunlight flood the room, and stepped into the hall to pour a cup of tea, nearly bumping into Timmy, Bull Ring Inn's owner.

"Morning, Miss O'Connor! Slept well, I trust? Your breakfast, I'm afraid, is simple fare today. I've just been called for an early departure on the ferry...winds picking up over the sea on the Wales side."

"Oh, that sounds like a possible storm coming this way?"

"Very possibly, and the workers don't want to get stranded over in Wales, so we adjust our days to suit the weather. Sorry about not having a full breakfast for you."

"Ah, well," Maggie said, "We'll plan to see you early this evening...we'll be out exploring again. And I don't mind getting my own breakfast...you've been wonderful to us."

"Mr. Loftus is already in the kitchen," he said as he turned to leave.

With that she scrambled back to bed, crawling back under the still-warm covers, taking her laptop and tea with her. At the signal of awaiting mail, her expectant hopefulness transformed into pleasure and she immediately opened the folder. She laughed as she read Thomas's stream of emails from Cavan, astonished by his report of their unwitting proximity, her good cheer fully restored. They were so charmingly pathetic! And so ridiculous...how could she say no?

She wished Jane were here right now. If she tried to talk to Eamon he'd only discourage her. She should say no, she should stop this silliness now. But her adventuresome nature won out. She would meet him...yes, she would but under her own terms, and not until she was sure of herself. Not just out of curiosity, but because he had an endearing quality that made her want to be close to him. Sporting a coy grin, she wrote a brief response, then finished dressing for breakfast.

* * * * * *

TO: SubDude99

FROM: EZWriter

SUBJECT: Let's talk...

Dear Thomas,
We're in Wexford and tomorrow will head north toward Dublin. Eamon's a fine videographer and has a knack for finding the most beguiling sites to explore — I'll bet you'd like him, Thomas. Anyway, perhaps there'll be an opportunity for us to talk in Dublin?
Maggie

P.S. That song...I can hum it but can't remember the lyrics...kiss me each morning, dada dum dada dada dum...is that how it goes?

She carefully omitted a reference to actually meeting him.

* * * * * *

The next morning they said their farewells to Timmy and departed Wexford, heading north on R742 alongside the sea. As they wound their way down roads that led them east toward the water and then west and inland, Eamon jabbered non-stop with tales of his mischievous school days. Then he became serious as he shared grim recollections of the Troubles, beatings and assaults he had witnessed on the streets of Portadown and Belfast. He recalled the fervent pleadings by some clergy for peace, by others who ironically incited parish disturbances, and the twisted maneuverings of politicians and IRA leaders that led to one violent retaliation after another.

They heard news on the radio about two incidents the previous night in Belfast, violent confrontations, both resulting in deaths — one an obvious IRA style beating a short distance from Queens University. Maggie could see the tension in Eamon's eyes as he listened for familiar names and saw his shoulders relax only slightly at the announcement of unfamiliar names, the grief settling on his face like heavy gray clouds shrouding once lighter skies.

* * * * * *

Journal Entry — West Coast Ireland.

Although politics and religious relations are much more tolerant here in the Republic, and the Garda are more like your small town constable than the RUC, there are occasions one is reminded that the Troubles are only a couple years back. While entering the downtown of Wexford in the cold, rainy night, we came around a sharp bend and had to slow to a halt, stalling the car (for only the twentieth time).

Suddenly we realized the road had narrowed because there was an extra lane of vehicles — military — lining the street in front of a bank. My blood ran cold when in front of my headlights I suddenly saw a uniformed man aiming a machine gun at us, possibly suspecting we were deliberate-

ly blocking their van. It may have been that they were extra police called to duty because of recent robberies in several big institutions over the past week. Unlike the U.S., people here don't stop to rubberneck, and we quickly moved on.

Ballinesker by the sea in southeast Ireland is the closest spot to England and in past centuries was the target for invasion by the Normans and Vikings. The influence of their cultures shows in the very narrow main streets of towns, particularly Wicklow, which is 20,000 population and whose main street barely allows a milk truck to pass through. The sidewalks are just wide enough to walk single-file, and people walk side by side in the street and on the curb. Here you'll find the local chemist, victualer, jewelers, toy shop, stationer, bakery, confectioners, etc., all situated around the town square and tucked in among several big banks. You can stroll the beach by the Irish Sea, where the wind rearranges the topography of the high dunes by the minute and the stubborn whiskers of seagrass refuse to let the harsh winds lay them permanently flat.

Northward to Arklow, where you might lunch in a pub on the best shepherd's pie you'll ever find and wander along streets decorated for Christmas where holiday songs blare out over loudspeakers on street corners. Here again you'll find narrow, hilly winding streets, a memorial statue of Fr. Michael Murphy, one of the leaders in the 1798 Irish Rebellion, and a crowd of people bustling about with Christmas lists in hand.

Past Arklow you enter the Wicklow Mountains

and travel past stud farms, down roads overhung with boughs of big ancient trees, flanked by meadows with sheep and neatly kept farmsteads, thatched-roof cottages, and green hills with farm boundaries marked by hedges rather than fences.

In the Vale of Avoca, around a bend you discover the Meeting of the Waters, where a lovely, ivy-covered stone bridge crosses two rivers set in between the hills. Travel just beyond there to Rathdrum, birthplace of P.C. Parnell, (where the streets are even narrower!) and into Glendalough, a quiet little place nestled in the Wicklow Mountains. A lassie in the pub will advise you that you might be lucky enough to see snow tonight, which she says dresses the hills with a heavenly frosting and makes them even more beautiful to see.

* * * * * *

They stopped at a small guest house in Glendalough in the late afternoon. A young girl balancing an infant on her right hip showed them to modestly appointed rooms. Her mother must have been timid because, Maggie noticed, the older woman peeked around a corner at them, then quickly picked up a clothes basket and disappeared, not to be seen again.

Maggie wondered briefly if their presence raised questions and became the target of new conversation in the small villages through which they passed. Certainly their young hostess was taken with Eamon, blushing profusely when he addressed her, stammering out the usual information about the bath, the heater, and their accommodations. The companions settled in their rooms, leaving their adja-

cent doors open so they could chat while Maggie conducted her usual ritual of unpacking and lining up toiletries on
a small dresser at the foot of her bed.

"I'm off to the pub, Mags...an old friend who owes
me runs it."

"Well, try to be diplomatic with him, Eamon, and
don't get thrown out of the pub. I'm thirsty, too!" She
looked at her watch. "Just enough time for me to plug in
and check with George and Jane. I'll meet you there in a
few minutes?"

"Aye, but pet, my friend's a lass, make no mistake
about it, and I'm always on my most charming behavior
with the colleens!" He bowed with a flourish and swag-
gered out the door and down the street.

On her way to the pub to meet Eamon, she stopped
across the street at the tiny post office, where she wrote
and posted cards for Jane, Charlie, and her mother.

* * * * * *

Somewhere a few miles from the peaceful, hilly village, further east on the coast, three men sat around a table
in the kitchen of a shabby, dirty tugboat that had seen better days. They were talking heatedly. The boat rocked
roughly with the high winter waves, agitating stomachs
and testing tempers. One of the men, a tall, fortyish chap
dressed in a dark turtleneck, blue jeans, and a wool blazer,
stood up abruptly and paced the short space of the kitchen.
He pitched the remains of a half-finished mug of bitter
coffee into the sink and slammed the mug on the counter.
The other two men flinched.

"What do you mean, you've lost them?" he hurled the words at them.

The two men looked harassed, tired, and unkempt, wearing clothes that looked like they'd been slept in. They weren't in a mood to be hauled over the coals.

"Look here, they're not driving a direct route. One minute they're headed north and then all of a sudden she turns onto some rutty little path and you can't even see ahead of you more than twenty meters!"

"Your job - your whole, simple, fucking job — is to maintain a proper surveillance. How hard can that be?"

The bigger of the two hired hands, a redhead with a ruddy complexion, scraped his chair back across the wood floor and leaned forward as if he might get up and take on the visitor. His neck flared almost as red as his hair from his anger. "Look, don't get fucking wise-ass on us. As soon as we catch up with them — and we will — we'll put a bug in their car."

"Well, I can tell you right now, Walker won't stand for shoddy work. He wants to know where Loftus is every second. The phone call between him and his connection has Walker concerned. What about your blokes following the American?"

"They're on him. And it's looking from his emails like he might be meeting up with the woman before too long."

"Well, don't lose him, and keep me posted every two hours." The tall man didn't wait for a response but turned and climbed up the short steps to topside. The two ruffians listened to his footsteps across the deck of the boat.

"Aye-aye, *Capitan*, sir," the smaller man hissed.

* * * * * *

She missed her daily communications with Thomas and wished she could hear his voice, even briefly, to fill in another of the blanks in her profile of him. If only she'd written down the phone number he emailed her. Impulsively, then, she picked up the public phone outside the post office and dialed the operator. "Could you give me the number for Cavan Arms, please." Quickly she scribbled down the number, said thanks, clicked down the receiver to hang up, and let it pop up again. She inserted some coins and dialed the number. *Don't even think about what you're doing or you'll hang up,* she told herself, *be adventurous!*

Having given in to her impulse, anticipating with a thrill the moment she would talk with him voice to voice, she was disappointed to learn from the hotel receptionist that Thomas had checked out of the hotel. *Drat*, she thought, *I miss him, I do.* And the acute longing she felt with this revelation startled her.

Maggie crossed back over to the bed and breakfast and sent an email to tell him of their whereabouts and their plans to drive cross-country to Galway. Looking at the map, she calculated they were less than two hours from Dublin. Perhaps she could try calling him again when they got there, but would he be in Dublin or Cavan, and damn it, why didn't he tell her where he'd be staying in Dublin?

Half an hour later, their thirst abated and restless to stretch their legs, Maggie and Eamon hiked up the road from the village to Glendalough to search for the site where the missionary hermit St. Kevin's remains were buried on the edge of the upper lake hundreds of years ago.

* * * * * *

Journal Entry — Glendalough.

Glendelough is the site of what, hundreds of years ago, had been a magnificent monastic settle-ment of several churches, a cathedral, round tower, school, and several other buildings. It was established by St. Kevin in the sixth century and was the destiny of pilgrims from that time forward.

The ruins are set between Upper and Lower Glendelough ("glen of two lakes"), in a valley couched between mountains where the mist clings to the rocks and trees and the fog rolls over the peaks like tumbleweed. It's isolated, ethereal, and inspires a quiet awe in its beauty.

The view is remarkable and the water on the lake like a mirror. We hiked around the main park area, completely alone except for the sheep roam-ing freely about the grounds.

The sheep are marked with either blue or red patches of some sort of dye, and I wondered whether the coloring denoted ownership or some-thing else. Eamon, I asked, what are the sheep painted for? Ah, he wisecracked, that tells the girls from the boys, lass. I should have known better than to ask such a question of a city boy. (I learned later that neighbors let their sheep graze together, and the markings do, after all, denote ownership.)

At any rate, the sheep appeared unimpressed with us and continued their contented grazing and occasional bleating. Cautiously Eamon crept up to them again and again, never getting closer than five feet away before they'd huff a cloud of steamy breath and retreat a short distance. He played with them — or were they playing with him? — holding his hand out as if to offer a treat and thinking he'd fool them the way he could his dog, Morgan.

I sat in a dry, sheltered cove of earth watching the steam of their breath float outward, hover, and dissipate as it blended with the misty air. It looked to me to be a piece of the magic of this place.

As dusk began to turn to night, we sat at the edge of the shore of Upper Lake near St. Kevin's Cell, a beehive-shaped structure where legend tells us St. Kevin lived as a hermit. There we contemplated the history of this quiet place. Surveying the banks of the lake through my binoculars, I spied two gray goats and two chocolate coated rams ambling along a rocky, uneven path around a bend across the lake. Straining against the darkening light, I noticed one ram was missing a leg and hobbled like an old soldier, while the others moved along at a very slow pace to accommodate their crippled companion. Or perhaps they rambled along so slowly because they're as entranced with the aura of Glendalough as I am. An unforgettable place...simply unforgettable.

* * * * * *

The next morning Thomas read Maggie's note. By the time he answered, however, she had checked her email and found a disappointingly empty mailbox, and now she and Eamon were dodging traffic in the early morning Dublin work rush hour on the choked thoroughfare of O'Connell

Street, searching for a parking spot. Thomas had sent his email too late.

TO: EZWriter

FROM: SubDude99

SUBJECT: Lunch on the Liffey

Maggie, dearest...
*   I'll be in Dublin this afternoon...will you be there waiting for me? I'll meet you at Kitty O'Shea's on Upper Canal Street. I'd be honored if you'll join me for lunch.*

He waited for a response as long as he could, then finally gave up and crossed the bridge over the River Liffey to walk the short distance to Trinity University. The professor had asked Thomas to meet him at his office so the Irishman could show him the university's famous library with its hall of busts, thousands of centuries-old books, and the most revered volume in Irish history, the intricately illustrated Book of Kells. That evening he would stay with the Professor in his apartment across from Trinity, and the following morning he would return to London for the meetings Philip had arranged. The next few days after that, his time was his own, and he meant to spend them in the company of one Maggie...Maggie what? He didn't even know her last name!

He had no way of knowing that all that morning Maggie and Eamon had been within blocks of him, recording the sights of Dublin, meandering through St. Stephen's

Green, listening to a street musician play "Scarborough Fair" on his homemade instrument.

But while he strolled across the courtyard at Trinity with the Professor, he felt a certain sense that she was thinking about him at that moment; and indeed she was, wondering what size he wore as she selected Christmas gifts of sweaters at Blarney Woolen Mills and walked back with Eamon across the River Liffey through throngs of shoppers for a late lunch at Bewley's on Grafton Street.

* * * * * *

Closing on midnight, Maggie and Thomas logged online within seconds of each other.

SubDude99: Maggie!

EZWriter: Thomas!

SubDude99: Where are you?"

EZWriter: Dublin...where are you?

SubDude99: Dublin! I'm in Dublin! You didn't get my email?

EZWriter: Nothing there at 5:30 this morning just before we left. You wrote?

SubDude99: Yes! Maggie, let me come over to wherever you are.

EZWriter: No.

SubDude99: Then will you meet me for coffee?

EZWriter: Yes.

SubDude99: You will???

EZWriter: Just not yet. And with a few conditions.

SubDude99: You prefer milk over cream?

EZWriter: (frowning)

SubDude99: When then?

EZWriter: Soon.

SubDude99: I can wait.

EZWriter: I'm heading west for a few days and want to be back in County Cavan next week for Christmas...

EZWriter: And I'll be with Eamon.

SubDude99: (frowning)

EZWriter: Also...

SubDude99: Also?

EZWriter: Also you must promise that you will be totally cool.

SubDude99: Natch. Unfortunately I am a gentleman first.

EZWriter: Unfortunately?

SubDude99: Being a gentleman doesn't sound like a handicap?

EZWriter: (grin)

SubDude99: When, Maggie?

EZWriter: Thursday — how about 3:30?

SubDude99: Today's Tuesday...I don't know if I can wait.

EZWriter: Forget it then.

SubDude99: Thursday, great. Half-three, as they say here. Where?

EZWriter: Cunningham's Bookstore on High Street in Galway.

SubDude99: Galway?

EZWriter: Aye (smiling)...I have to pick up a special book for my nephew Charlie, and they're supposed to have a copy there.

SubDude99: Maggie....

EZWriter: Yes, Thomas?

SubDude99: What's your last name?

EZWriter: O'Connor. I tried to phone you yesterday. What's yours?

SubDude99: deFremond. You did? Maggie?

EZWriter: Yes, Thomas?

SubDude99: When we meet in Galway....

SubDude99: if you're disappointed...

EZWriter: Half-three in Galway. Don't be late. Good night, Thomas. Sleep tight. {{**}}

With that, Maggie logged off. She felt flushed and warm. One thing at a time, she thought. She didn't want to think about disappointment. She hoped they were both above that physical attraction thing, anyway. Yeah, right. Anyway, he wouldn't disappoint her, she was sure of that, and what could she disapprove of, his lack of neatness? Big deal. She already knew he touched her in a place deep inside that no one had touched before. And it felt wonderful. And she didn't want to think about the possibility that he'd be disappointed in her.

chapter 7

GALWAY

Galway City

Nervously she checked her watch. Three-ten. Every-thing was cold and wet and the air felt thick with a fine drizzle. The cobble streets shone with a greasy wet coat, and lights were flickering on in stores earlier than usual against the darkening gray December afternoon. Flocks of umbrellas bobbed up and down the street, and Maggie thought how deftly these people walked about their business without bumping and poking each other. As for herself, she had to watch her step on the narrow side-walks and dodge the crowds, occasionally hearing a "sorry?" as people politely stepped around her.

Gradually her pace blended with the flow and she was able to look about her. Quaint shops with colorful facades spaced between restaurants, bakeries and pubs lined nar-row, winding lanes. Window displays, behind large plates of glass with intricate gold lettering spelling out the pro-prietor's name, boasted fine china, lace and silver, jewelry and art from England, France, and Germany.

Looking down the street over the wave of shoppers,

she noticed a continuous row of quaint, brightly painted signs swinging to and fro above shop doors and took out her camera to shoot them. In her lens she caught sight of Eamon a few yards ahead of her, videotaping and drawing a following of curious onlookers. She smiled and waved to him. He grinned and shrugged. *The Irish definitely have an affinity with the arts*, she thought, *and this videography captivates them.* They welcomed any opportunity to be part of cinema, and Eamon grandly played Peter Pan to their curiosity.

She checked her watch again and looked at the street sign...Main. She signaled to Eamon, who untangled himself from a group of boisterous youngsters and joined her. Together they headed toward High Street to look for Cunningham's Books and Maps. Once there, standing across the street looking at the place she was beginning to think might lead to her destiny, Maggie hesitated. She frowned, unsure, and glanced at Eamon, who shrugged again and smiled, his eyes promising her everything would be all right.

"It's your idea, pet. You'll be fine. I'll be nearby if you need me." He seemingly turned his attention back to the street and his surroundings. Maggie knew, though, that she would never be out of his sight.

She crossed the street to Cunningham's and looked around, wondering if Thomas was one of these people, if he was within feet or yards or blocks of her. Unable to detect his presence in any of the faces she scanned, she gave up her futile search and focused on the store. Standing outside the shop on the narrow pavement, she peered through the huge filmy window at the stacks of books set haphazardly about the store.

A cluttered room crammed with volumes of books and periodicals in every shape, size, color and age, the tables had been arranged with barely passable aisles to give books preference over customers. The perimeter of the store was lined with shelves from floor to the twelve-foot ceilings. In a corner toward the back of the shop, a high, wide cabinet with rows and rows of shallow drawers stood in front of a table on which maps of various sizes were scattered. A heavy desk lamp topped by a leaded glass shade provided light for an elderly man poring over a map with a magnifying glass. Other people browsed the treasure troves of shelves, and a couple of others formed a queue, waiting to have their purchases rung up by the clerk.

Shaking the rain from her umbrella, Maggie stepped through the door to admire the creaking wood plank floors, the ladders with wheels, the hand-lettered labels for subject sections. She took pleasure in the mingling smells of old paper, ink, wood, and even the mustiness. Normally obsessive about tidiness, Maggie's love of books prevailed and she smiled with approval. *Nope, I wouldn't change a thing...well,* she mused, *maybe I'd straighten up a shelf or two.*

The proprietor, a scholarly looking woman wearing reading glasses on a chain and a baggy navy blue sweater, walked over to her.

"Might I be of assistance?"

"Oh, yes, please! I'm looking for a book that will interest my fifteen-year-old nephew. He's really into ancient architecture."

"That would be over here, in this section." The woman shrugged to straighten her sweater, pushed her glasses back up on her nose, and led Maggie to a corner near the front of the store. "Anything on these shelves might work for you."

"Thanks, I'll take a look."

"You sound American?"

"Yes, I am, from Minnesota."

"Minnesota? Would that be in the south?"

"No," Maggie smiled. Nobody in Ireland ever seemed to know where Minnesota was...they could tell you exactly how to get to their cousin's house in Brooklyn but they usually think Minnesota is part of Canada. "Minneapolis, that's my town."

"Oh! My son's friend owns a pub there...Kieran's, I believe it's called."

"Yes, I know that place...it's wonderful!"

"Well, then, perhaps someday when you're there you'll tell Jack Manahan the Cunninghams are thinking of him and wishin' him well."

"I'll do that."

"Well, I'll leave you to look for your book...if you need help, please give me a wave, will you?"

"Yes, I will, and thank you."

She turned back to the shelves and found a book almost immediately. She thumbed through *Castles of the Midlands* and could picture Charlie becoming absorbed in its pages. After paying for it, Maggie nodded to the proprietor and stepped outside, recalling again her primary reason for being there. She looked around again and seeing no one approaching, she turned back toward the shop to resume her window browsing.

* * * * * *

Thomas cursed. Damn, he'd forgotten his umbrella in the car. He ducked into stores along High Street to avoid the steady shower. Finally, exasperated and nearly soaked, he relented and bought an umbrella, chastising himself for stubbornly holding out.

Brushing beads of rain from his coat and armed with his new "brellie", he ventured back up High Street until he saw the bold block letters of Cunningham's Books and Maps high above the awning. He scanned the crowd and almost immediately saw her...he was sure of it. He stood on the curb across the two-lane street, hooded by his umbrella and, over the roofs of passing cars, studied her from behind.

She was of medium height, perhaps five-six or five-seven, and it seemed two-thirds of that must be legs clad in black tights and clunky shoes. A short plaid skirt peaked out below a black slicker, and the gloved hands held an umbrella in one hand and a parcel in the other. Three fingers and the thumb of the right glove had holes and her fingers poked out from the tips. Thomas squinted, tried vainly to see the detail in the fingers, but he was too far away. Curly brown hair was tied back loosely under a wool hat, much of it escaping the ribbon and sticking out tousled from under the hat. She seemed to be engrossed in looking at the window display, and she fidgeted, lightly stomping a foot, crossing her legs, then stood straight and hugged herself briefly to fend off the wet chill. When she looked at her watch, he reflexively looked at his, too. Three twenty-eight.

He shifted his gaze to her reflection in the window. Though he couldn't see fine details, he was drawn to the sparkle in her eyes, apparent even in the dullness of the darkened window mirror, and he willed this woman to be Maggie. He was transfixed. He could have stood there watching her a long time; but the eyes in the reflection moved and met his, flickered away, and turned back for a fleeting moment to catch his gaze again. Her eyes narrowed as if squinting to see the man in the glass better. She turned to look behind her, locating him across the street, then turned away in embarrassment. It hadn't occurred to her at first that the tall stranger was staring at her.

She looked across the street toward Eamon, stepping backward toward the doorway and searching for a few moments to make sure he was within sight. Finally spotting him in a courtyard between two buildings watching her, she smiled nervously, waved and spun away into the doorway. She ran right into the stranger's chest, bumping her chin into something hard and sharp sticking out from his coat pocket. They were crunched together in the skinny opening.

"Ow!"

"So sorry! Please, allow me." Why he did it, he couldn't imagine, but Thomas feigned a clipped British accent and carefully moved to one side to make space for her to step through the doorway.

"I was ...I was just going to..." Bashfulness overcame her and she looked down at her shoes, shaking her head at her own nervousness. She cleared her throat and tried again. "I think we should try this again."

"After you, m'lady." Thomas bowed with a flourish, feeling chivalrous and foolish at the same time. Why had he assumed this absurd accent?

Maggie had regained her composure. She looked sideways at Thomas, raised her eyebrows, then surprised him with a mock curtsey.

"Pretty gallant...for an American." Smug, she was. Not fooled by the fool. He grinned sheepishly.

Back inside the bookstore, she unlatched her umbrella, leaned outside to shake off the loose rain, then closed it and swiveled directly into him again. *Get out of my way buster*, she thought, *you're messing things up here*. But he kept his eyes locked on hers, and she returned the scrutiny.

It struck her then. *Thomas?* she asked but the name was unspoken, no sound escaped her mouth. She glanced at the clock in the bookstore — three-thirty — and looked back at him. He was nothing at all like the countless faces she had drawn in her mind. From half a foot below him, she looked up toward his face to see that his green eyes were hooded with short, thick lashes and reddish-brown brows. Set between them, his nose was neat and rather nondescript except for a dimple at the tip. Maggie quickly scrutinized his mouth...masculine, bit of a contradictory smirk. Overall, a nice-looking face.

He lifted his hand to his head, self-consciously smoothing his rumpled, graying auburn hair, and her eyes inadvertently followed the motion...big hands, a little rough, big knuckles, no jewelry, neatly trimmed nails.

Thomas. She didn't want to stop looking at him, registering every detail.

Neither could he turn his gaze away from her. High cheekbones made more prominent by a warm flush, a high forehead, a little on the skinny side, fine boned. Raspberry lips, fair skin, and those eyes...violet, deep, clear, sparkling violet. He'd never seen eyes like those, darkly fringed and clear, like the deep violet blue of a tanzanite gem. From her bangs, thick, unruly strands of hair hung too low over her eyes, making her blink.

Without thinking he reached up and gently pushed her hair out of the way for her and smiled. His fingertips on her brow sent a warm rush through her, and she immediately wanted to feel that touch again. Without realizing it, she leaned toward him, smiling tentatively, her eyes asking him to do that again. It didn't occur to her until hours later that this was an abnormal reaction for her. Typically her reflexive response to a strange man's touch was cool withdrawal. Not this time, not with him.

At that moment Eamon appeared, standing in the doorway. He coughed to get their attention and frowned when neither noticed. Scowling, he stepped into the shop, assuming the stance of a patron intent on finding a certain book, but never allowing sight of them to vanish from his visual perception. He strained to hear their conversation.

Thomas backed away a respectful distance and dropped the unconvincing accent. "Got me — American through and through. Are you looking for something in particular?"

"Uh...yeah...yes...I was looking for a gift for my nephew, but..."

Nephew...you are *Maggie...yes!* He fought to maintain a straight face.

"Here..." he pulled a book of poetry from the brimming shelves, "I think you'll like this."

She looked at him questioningly, opened the slim volume, and leafed through it.

"I've never heard of Dermot Healy. Sorry...I don't think this is quite his style, and actually, I've already found something."

"Well then, please let me get this for you. A souvenir from one American tourist to another, but under one condition."

"Which is?"

"You must have a cup of coffee — or tea, anyway — with me, Maggie." The charade was up. Her flush deepened.

"Thomas?...Thomas." He nodded once, watching her. She smiled broadly, and those vexing tears glistened again, giving away her thrill. "I, uh, I saw a...a coffee shop down the street." Finally her eyes left his and she looked in the direction her hand was pointing, then back at him. Damn, she wanted to be cool, but this was a bit overwhelming. She wanted to bypass the formalities, felt an urge instead to kiss him, feel his arms around her, hugging her, but her reserve held her back.

She had anticipated that seeing him would change things. She wasn't prepared, however, for the physical reaction that was flowing through her. *Be cool*, she admonished herself, as electrical charges of impressions and reactions surged through her brain. *He's just a man, another person, a complete stranger...well, sort of...for Pete's sake, calm down...but oh, his touch...do I shake his hand? hug him? Stand here like dumb cluck?* A tingling pain reminded her of her sore chin and she reached up to rub the pain away.

"Oh, does it hurt? I am sorry...but it's really your fault. This was your idea." He looked down, reached into his coat, and pulled out a rumpled brown bag twisted around a square box, and looked back at her. Their eyes lingered on each other, talking for them, saying words and expressing thoughts too complex to comprehend. The real words they said kept them on an even keel. The conversation with their eyes mystified and perplexed them both. Each of them having prepared for disappointment, certainly neither expected this powerful physical attraction. They both were trying to dismiss the reaction, unsure if the other could be feeling the same depth of excitement. Subconsciously their expressions conveyed their feelings to each other.

He opened the bag and pulled out the box. She looked at it and laughed. "You remembered." She held out her hand and he set the Tobler chocolate into her palm. "Alright! This will be delicious with tea."

"I remember, of course, the explicit instructions that one must whack the orange thoroughly in order to crack it open and release the delectable taste? Is that it?" He looked into her eyes with such genuine desire to get it right that she laughed again.

"Yes, exactly...just a little bit like life in general...sometimes, first you have to break issues wide open before you can appreciate the pleasure life has to offer." She recalled Eamon and their moments back in Killykeen Forest, his gentle way of cracking open her long-protected wall. She looked around and found him. He nodded, and she waved to him to come over.

"Eamon Loftus...Thomas deFremond." The men shook hands coolly at first, then simultaneously tightened their grip, swiftly sizing each other up. Oblivious to the exertion of masculine natural response to competition, Maggie smiled happily from one to the other and shrugged a cheerful sigh. It took her a few seconds of silence to realize that everyone in the trio wasn't pleased.

"Well...well. Well! Eamon! Thomas! I believe I've mentioned to you that Eamon is from Belfast. We're working together on a documentary...oh yeah, I've told you about that, haven't I? Anyway, Eamon is an extraordinary photographer, and we've been working very hard on this. Isn't that right, Eamon?"

"Aye." Eamon wasn't helping the conversation to flow.

"And we're making wonderful progress, isn't that right?"

"Aye."

"And Eamon is quite a charming fellow really, aren't you?"

Silence.

"Yes, well then, Eamon, we're going to Hafferty's for a spot of tea. I saw it back about a block...okay?" The lack of an invitation to accompany them blazed across her words.

"Well then...aye. I saw a camera shop up the lane. I need a lens. You won't mind if I join up with you later?"

"Fine, terrific." Maggie looked hard at him, imploring him to understand. His return glare wasn't reassuring.

"Fine. I'll meet up with you at Hafferty's in awhile." Eamon did understand, he just didn't like it. He didn't like the way her eyes sparkled and the way her face glowed more than before. He glowered at Thomas, then quickly turned and left the pair, disappearing out the door and up the street.

* * * * * *

The orange foil wrap of the Tobler chocolate lay spread open with wedges fanned out. A contented smile rested on Maggie's lips as, with eyes closed, she slowly sucked on an orange-flavored chocolate wedge.

Thomas watched, mesmerized by her expression. It seemed to him that everything she felt, every emotion her brain generated was registered on her face. There seemed to be nothing secretive about her. Her simple openness bewildered Thomas, who was more accustomed to poker-faced business dealings and having to excavate hidden agendas in the people he associated with in the industry. Yet as she met his gaze briefly, he recognized something enigmatic, something pained and vulnerable. He realized then that up to now, through their online exchanges, however revealing, he'd only glimpsed the surface of her.

They sat at a small, wobbly wrought iron table in front of the window. A candle lamp took up much of the space, and the Tobler orange and teacups on saucers consumed the rest. The dainty matching chairs were built for petite frames, and Thomas shifted uncomfortably, almost knocking his chair over. The grating scrape of the chair legs on the floor disrupted Maggie's chocolate reverie. She opened her eyes and looked directly at Thomas, smiling again.

"Well, you certainly have a knack for cracking open these chocolate oranges," he said.

"I've had practice."

"You weren't sure you could trust me...is that why you brought Eamon along?"

"No, not really...not totally. We're working together on the documentary, he needs to be here, you knew that." Flustered at having been caught behaving cautiously, Maggie blushed and defensively added, "Okay, okay! So I wasn't absolutely sure of you. Can you blame me? What if you were a...a serial killer or something? What if you were...oh, I don't know — you never know what sort of crazy person you'll meet on the Internet." She winced with the realization of what she'd just said, a recital of Jane's frequent admonitions.

"A bodyguard, ah...I see. Good thinking, Miss O'Connor."

"Thomas, I can't just rush into something like this."

"No, you should let the tea cool a little first." His droll tone annoyed her. She set down her cup of tea and stared into it. This was going miserably.

"You know what I mean...meeting a complete stranger in a strange way."

"Excuse me? I didn't think we were strangers."

"Listen...this was a mistake. I think I should leave. I have a documentary to produce." Suddenly feeling foolish, she stood up, preparing to flee. He was just another damned male trying to take advantage of her, and she would have none of it. He reached over the table and held her forearm to stop her. She tried to pull back. Thomas hung onto her firmly, then softened his grip, his eyes asking for pardon. She stopped resisting and looked at him hard. After hesitating a moment, she sat down again, her sensitive pride wounded. His hand moved down her arm and gently rested on top of her hand, patting it softly. Tenderly he placed her hand in his and began to examine it while she watched.

"Delicate hands you have, Maggie O'Connor. Listen to me...I won't ask you to rush into anything. But we know each other well, we've said a lot in our letters and our conversations that told more than the words we wrote. I know this...I don't have to rush into anything because I'm already where I want to be. You're my friend, and I want to be close to you."

The sincerity in his voice reassured her, and she knew she felt the same way. She relaxed again.

"I'm only here for the day. Eamon and I are leaving for the Connemaras early tomorrow morning."

"Then let me come with you, Maggie...let me finish some work, and let me come with you for a couple days. I can be ready tomorrow morning by, say, nine thirty. I've got a car."

"And what about Eamon?"

"What about Eamon?"

"Our itinerary, deadlines. He'll be filming while I'm interviewing and narrating."

"Maggie, for three days couldn't you work alone?"

It occurred to her then that this might be a one-time opportunity. She thought for only a moment longer.

"Thomas, I do want to spend time with you. There's so much I want to share with you, talk about. But if you're coming with me, so is Eamon."

"Alright, alright," he conceded. "I understand. But let's take two cars." She nodded.

"We can do that. Let me talk to him."

"Nine-thirty then?"

"Eight-thirty. Pick me up at the Inishmore Guesthouse on the road to Salthill so we can get to the docks in time for the boat to the Arans."

Thomas saluted her. "Aye, captain! More tea?" He'd have to hustle to finish his work and be ready, but he wouldn't miss this opportunity to be with her.

* * * * * *

Eamon spoke in a hushed tone on the hallway phone.

"Yes, I've met the fellow. Maggie says he's here to negotiate for the rights to produce an Irish invention in the States. No, I'm not sure yet how much more she knows but I should find out shortly. I have a feeling we're going to be seeing quite a bit of him. Okay, I'll be in touch. Right." He hung up just as Maggie walked in the door.

"Who's that, your mother? Remember you promised to call her."

"Me ma? No, darlin', 'twas an old flame...she can't get over me...but I told her you're my number one girl now."

Maggie feigned a flattered look. "Well then, number one guy, shouldn't you be taking me out for a bite to eat?"

"There's a pub not far from here. Are you up for a walk?"

"Sure. Sounds great."

On the road to the pub, Maggie chattered about Galway before leading up to what she really wanted to talk about.

"Eamon, it's lovely here. You have the best of everything close by...city culture, picturesque countryside. No matter where you look everything is magical and beautiful."

"Professionally trained militants, fireworks and bombs, poverty, tension, fear, pessimism. Yup, we've got it all, and it can be delivered right to your doorstep."

"Not everywhere, Eamon. You can't hope to cure the ails of hundreds of years of dissension, but in spite of the Troubles, the Irish are a gentle people. You're a prime example, you know."

"Aye, Mags, so'tis. I love my country. But many Irish have never set foot outside their country and have nothing to compare it with. Now then, stop tryin' to divert the conversation. Tell me about him."

Direct. She couldn't fault him for that, she liked it when people were square with her. "What would you like to know? I met him online, you knew that. I told him we were here. Now we've met. He's doing something here for an American computer company."

"I thought you said he worked for a British company?"

"The company he works for is owned by a British company. He was in London on business and then he came here and sort of got sidetracked into chasing down an Irish inventor."

"What did this inventor invent?"

"Some sort of a crystal screen for a computer. Thomas is checking it out on the chance his company might want to back it. He's quite excited about the potential. He says it could 'put Ireland on the technology map.' He didn't say anything more about it. Eamon, please keep this quiet, okay?"

"What does he mean, it could put Ireland on the technology map? If a British company makes it, England would steal the glory of it, and where would that leave Ireland?"

"Just wait till you talk to him, Eamon. Thomas is a

visionary. I think he sees a bigger picture than his British associates do. He sees it as a way that Ireland can create a non-polluting industry that could impact the world's economic structure. All the raw materials, he says, are local. All the labor force for the plant could easily be found here."

"He doesn't want to just buy the idea and take it back home?"

"No, he's adamant that if he pursues it, he'll ensure it's developed as a product of the Republic of Ireland. Anyway, Thomas has a meeting with this professor next week. He asked me to go with him."

Eamon looked thoughtful, absorbing this information. He needed to make sure it got to the right people. He changed the subject.

"Hey, I'm miserable starvin'. Here's the pub. Let's get some grub, as you Westerners say."

* * * * * *

He took the news poorly about Thomas joining them for the trek across to the Aran Islands. What Eamon particularly protested, however, was taking separate cars and possibly going their separate ways.

"We've got a job to do, Maggie, and I'm not keen on breaking up our schedule like this."

"We'll keep working and we'll stay on schedule. I'm not forgetting what we're here for. He'll be along for the ride. He won't get in the way, Eamon...maybe he can even help with a fresh perspective."

"Well then, we can easily fit into one car. I'll ride in the back."

"Right, in these tiny cars, with your long legs? You'd

be getting cramps inside ten kilometers. No Eamon. I want — I *need* a couple days with him."

"Great, brilliant. What happened to 'number one guy?'"

"I guess I'm just a little fickle." Her voice was tight. She spoke through an even smile. "Can't you just go on ahead and shoot some footage yourself? I'll be right behind, and we can compare notes and film in a couple days."

"Maggie, we're supposed to be a team. This isn't the kind of job that you just splice together after I do my part and you do yours. We have to see the same things, experience them together if the story's gonna have any cohesion to it."

Her grim silence warned Eamon to leave it alone.

"Fine. But I'm not leavin' you alone with this bloke. I'm following right behind you."

Overcoming his anxiety about driving was a sacrifice and Maggie knew it, but he had made her angry. She bristled and turned away from him. She snapped a cold reply over her shoulder.

"Fine."

"Fine."

chapter 8

THE WILD WEST

Aran Islands, County Galway

Thomas pulled up in front of the Inishmore Hotel at eight-fifteen a.m. Maggie, anxious to be on the road, had her bags sitting on the walk in front of the door. She was fidgeting, periodically peering through a slit in the lace curtains of her second floor front room window, pacing, anxiously watching for him. Hearing the change of gears as his Opal turned the corner, she practically knocked Eamon over in the hallway as she flew down the steps to the front entryway. Out of breath at the bottom, she halted, checked her hair in the mirror hanging by the door, calmed herself and then leaned out and waved.

"G'morning! You're early! I'll be just a second, okay?"

"Are these your bags? I'll get them loaded." She nodded and smiled.

Thomas got out of the car and started to load her bags. She paused, watching him, smiling, then closed the door and turned around to see Eamon coming down the stairs. A sulky countenance marred his handsome face.

"Aw, come on, Eam, it's a sunny day. We're lucky it's

not raining! This'll be fun! The hills should be gorgeous."
Determined to enjoy the day, she settled the bill with the
innkeeper and then, passing Eamon as he held the door
open, she stretched up on her toes and kissed him on the
cheek. She made faces at him until he responded and made
a face back at her. Quickly she hugged him tightly.

"See ya at the ferry, Sweetie."

"Aye, Lass." She bounced out the door, ignoring the
bite in his voice.

* * * * * *

The wind chasing the ocean waves whipped against
their faces and tore at their clothes. The ferry was a small
one, holding just a half dozen cars and their passengers
along with skids of provisions for the few stores and
homes on the Aran Islands. The crossing was cold despite
the sunshine. Maggie huddled the men close to her on
either side to keep warm while they rode the swells and
leaned with the sway of the boat. As the ferry approached
Inisheer on the southern end of the island group, she
looked due south with her binoculars and spotted the Cliffs
of Moher in far-off County Clare across the South Sound.
It was a spectacular sight with the sun dancing off shadows of clouds, blanketing the craggy rock and wind-swept
pasture above. She glanced at Eamon, who had already
pulled out his camera and was focusing on the cliffs.

Stepping off the ferry, they were struck by the rugged,
bare beauty of the Arans and the ruddy faces of the
islanders that testified to their hardy lifestyle. As forbidding as the islands looked from the sea, their magnificent
angles and contours supplied Eamon's photographic

appetite with ample footage. He set to work immediately, planning his strategy to capture in his lens the challenge of life on these primitive shores.

For this leg of the trip, ferrying out to the Arans, the threesome agreed to travel in one car, and their day together served to suspend the open animosity between Thomas and Eamon. In fact, each man was likable and generally enjoyed an easy camaraderie with other men. By the end of the day, each had to grant that the other fellow was a worthy chap. In fact, where Maggie wasn't concerned, they found much in common, and where Maggie was concerned, they developed an armistice of sorts from their mutually protective feelings for her.

Throughout the day Thomas observed the two journalists in action, admiring the manner in which they worked together. They conducted their work as if they'd known each other always, in the way they examined and chronicled their observations through naturally attuned views with the complementary media of video and written word. He noticed what they took for granted — an unconstrained bond that lent graceful dynamics to their work, a synergy that normally only seasoned journalistic teams enjoy.

Thomas riddled Eamon with questions about Ireland's recent industrial and economic development, and the two men talked at length about technology and Ireland's capacity for growth. Finally, Thomas spoke comfortably with Eamon about his reasons for being there and confided to Eamon his interest in the professor's device, discreetly leaving out the details of Pennton's identity and the actual characteristics of his invention. Surprised that Thomas would trust him with even this general information about his mission, Eamon reciprocated with names of contacts in Dublin who could help Thomas maneuver through government regulations to establish an American-Irish partnership. Thomas sensed an ally in Eamon and trusted that his gut instinct wasn't misguided.

For Eamon's part, he reluctantly but fairly acknowledged privately an acceptance of Thomas, gradually realizing the other man's genuine intentions and feelings for Maggie. One couldn't ignore the chemistry between Thomas and Maggie. Uncharacteristically, Eamon subconsciously resolved to step back and give them space. If nothing developed, or even if it did, he'd be there for Maggie. He'd love her in any way she'd let him.

* * * * * *

Hours later, the three of them warmed by the purchases of Aran wool sweaters designed and hand-knitted by the wives of three fisherman they'd met, Eamon drove the Opal off the ferry and back onto the mainland at Rossaveal just as the sun began to set on the western horizon, silhouetting the islands. Maggie noticed his wide eyes and white knuckles as he climbed out of the car. She quietly motioned Thomas away and stepped over to stand next to Eamon. He faced away from her, staring straight ahead, not wanting her to detect his strung nerves.

"Eamon," she said gently, "You did wonderfully getting off the ferry, I'd think you'd been driving regularly for years.

"Aye, Mags, 'tis a breeze once you get the hang of it." He looked at her and managed a thin, weak smile, then looked away again.

They parked the car in the village square and got out for a stretch before resuming their journey across the Connemaras.

Hearing only the strange syllables of the Irish language

surrounding them as they entered a dark tavern, where warmth radiated from an enormous arched brick fireplace in the center of the floor, Maggie and Thomas turned to Eamon for translation. With grace he slipped into his Irish and ordered three stouts. Bantering with the barkeeper and customers, he watched with pleasure the ritual of drawing the Guinness and letting the foam settle. On the bet of an old man that he couldn't remember the Irish words to an old pub song, Eamon tentatively sang one verse and then, flipping a pound on the bar and nodding to the old man, laughingly stumbled his way through the next verse in English to the ready accompaniment of fiddle and drum.

As the other patrons picked up the song, Eamon discreetly studied the pair across the room. Enviously he watched their total absorption in each other, the way they leaned in closely to speak in hushed tones, the way Maggie sparkled and laughed at what Thomas was telling her, the way he scooped her hand between his and watched her with unabashed adoration. *Sickening,* he thought...*silly fookin' lovebirds they are.* Suddenly he felt quite lonely, unused to being odd man out. Turning back to the bar, he chatted with the patrons and barkeeper a few minutes more, then carried the three glasses of stout to the table where they were waiting.

"The fellows here say I can find an old school chum of mine up the road from here. You wouldn't mind if I run over to chat him up a bit and meet you later tonight in Clifden?"

"Uh...sure, fine by me. We'll find our way and meet you there in time for dinner. You know where we're staying, right?" Maggie looked at him thoughtfully. He nodded. He didn't return her look but rather turned the conversation to more anecdotes of his days as a student at

Queens. An hour later, while the others were talking with some of the villagers, he slipped out the door unnoticed.

* * * * * *

The thunderous crashing of the Atlantic waves against the rocks below greeted them as they passed Ballyconneely Bay and rounded the peninsula to arrive at Clifden late in the afternoon. Thomas drove leisurely down the main street and then up a hilly side lane and across another until he located the Clifden Arms, a medieval-looking inn with heavy wood doors, large black iron knobs and latches. Big windows facing the sheltered waters of Ardbear Bay allowed light to flood the lobby.

Despite the calmness of the bay, the harsh, icy Atlantic wind found its way over the hill and whipped between the streets and buildings of the town. Maggie was glad to get out of it and into the comfortable stillness of the inn.

She checked in and picked up the keys for their rooms, asked after Eamon and learned he hadn't yet shown up, then helped Thomas unload their overnight bags and equipment. Dropping their things in their rooms, they met again in the hallway. An awkward silence fell between them. Maggie quickly closed the door to her room and glanced nervously away from Thomas's room across the hall. Their eyes met and in one electric instant they read each other's minds. Flustered, Maggie turned and led the way down the stairs, willing her heart to slow down, her mind to think of anything else.

They strolled along the streets, window-shopping, visiting the bodhran craftsman and examining his work, then stepped next door into the woolen shop, where she bought a scarf for Jane and a wool blanket for herself. *This'll come in handy,* she thought, recalling the frosty nights since they'd left Belfast, where at least the radiators were kept heating most of the night.

Back out in the fading light and brisk air, they shared an easier silence, and as they walked along Maggie comfortably slipped her arm through Thomas's, matching his pace. The naturalness of her action pleased him. He gently squeezed her hand and drew her arm close against his side.

Suddenly she halted in front of a jeweler's display window. The gold of the rings, earrings, and chains resting on folds of deep burgundy velvet glittered in the brightly lit window. She looked across the rows of jewelry. Her gaze settled on a Claddagh ring, which she had read was a Gaelic symbol of eternal friendship, molded with two hands surrounding a heart topped with a crown. Its unusual style and broad symbolism appealed to her. Friendship, love, respect, admiration...these feelings were abstract in her mind, indefinable in that they could mean different things in the spectrum of relationships. The centuries old design seemed to represent every human bond in an all-encompassing expression. *What will it ever bring to me,* she wondered...*will I ever have romance with someone that I'd call my best friend, too?*

"Want to try one on?" He had no desire to shop, ever. But for her, he'd be patient, even cooperative.

"No," she smiled, coming out of her reverie, then blushed. It felt presumptive, a mistaken implication and inappropriate to stand here, looking at jewelry with a man she had only begun to know. Concerned that he might be reading her completely wrong, she nudged him and nodded down the street. "Let's have something to eat. I wonder if Eamon's here yet."

The Shoddy Hoof Pub stood between two tourist shops three blocks away, barely five minutes on foot, and the evening light and the gentle emergence of the luminous stars made the walk delightful. The wind had slowed to occasional light sweeping gusts and then calmness; the air carried with it the promise of a frigid night. As they walked arm in arm up the short hill from Market Street toward the pub, the salty smells of smoked salmon and sea air assailed their nostrils. Further up the street a truck with an open rack carrying crates swerved down the narrow road toward the bay, the only sign of life except for smoke curling out of chimneys and lights flickering through windows here and there.

Pausing at a small square on the edge of Market Street, barren of trees or shelter but adorned with two brightly painted benches, Maggie set her shopping bags down on one of them. She walked over to the squat stone wall bounding the square near the steep hill that sloped down to the bay. Below them, the bay looked desolate in its winter dress, deserted by the deep sea fishermen who maneuvered their boats out early in the morning and returned well after twilight. Most of the buildings along the water's edge stood dormant for the winter, and small boats bobbed lazily in their moorings side by side in the sheltered marina, creaking protests as they scraped against the docks.

"Why did you choose to come here now, Maggie? Summer would be a more likely time to do a travelogue of Ireland."

"First of all," stung by his inadvertent insult, labeling her work a "travelogue", she snapped, "Toulouse doesn't *do* travelogues. We produce features that examine the economy, the politics, the history of the land and the people, how the country fits in with the global scheme. Secondly, I wanted to do this story now, when tourists aren't invading the countryside."

Soundly chastised, Thomas recognized that her instincts were on target but couldn't pass up the merriment in arguing with her. The sparkle in her eyes and the flush in her cheeks flared when she was provoked.

"But Ireland doesn't have much else to offer other than tourism, so isn't that a critical element to your documentary?"

"Thomas, I can't believe you said that. Ireland's changing, it's progressing, and at the same time there are movements to preserve the elements that will help the country sustain its uniqueness ...the clean environment, the artistic culture, the tenacity of the people and how it's rooted in their history and religion and politics. That's the Ireland I want to reveal to the rest of the world."

Resolutely she spoke. Sincerity rang in the fervency of her voice and burned in the violet flame in her eyes. Thomas thought about his own mission and knew that they shared a similar motivation. Reflecting on what she'd said and the plans he had begun to conceive with the professor, he cemented his decision to pursue the development of the device with Ian Pennton.

They turned their backs to the stark, frigid bay and resumed their walk to the Shoddy Hoof. At the doorway they were greeted by the mingling smells of strong coffee, whiskey, burning peat, and cigarette smoke. Cheaply framed, dusty pictures of years of championship Connemara ponies lined the walls in the entrance. Inside, the tavern was like those in every other little hamlet in Connemara. Small lamps hanging on the walls above scratched, highly polished booths faintly lit the long narrow corridor that was the pub. A high bar on one side accommodated the patrons, who sat tending their drinks as they watched the bartender draw another Guinness and another after that.

A television loudly blared the news, glasses and dishes clattered in a kitchen somewhere beyond a door behind the bar, and from that same direction laughter and chatter between two women tumbled into the room. Barstools scraped on rough-hewn planks of timeworn oak smoothed by ages of patrons hoisting themselves up onto the high-legged stools.

Thomas led Maggie to a table across from the bar and held a chair out for her. She glanced at him, his arm grazing hers. She liked the feel of him close to her. She set down her bags and unzipped her jacket. He helped her out of it, brushing her shoulder as he pulled it off. A hint of her scent wafted across his path, filling his senses. Its light, lavender soap essence, mingling with the soft smell of her skin, sparked an urge deep inside him. He took a deep breath and memorized that scent. Leaning imperceptibly closer to her as she sat down, his hand reached up to touch her hair, running a finger through a cluster of curls, then enveloped her in his arms for one second as he slid her chair in, his cheek grazing her hair. Maggie felt it, as did he...the quickening pulse, the keen awareness of his presence merging with hers.

The plaintive, soulful sounds of a folk song emanated from a round booth near them, where a trio of locals had gathered to hobnob, drink and play their instruments, a violin, guitar, and bodhran. Elsewhere in the room, a quietness sifted like a cloud through the dusky night, and for a few minutes conversation ceased while everyone listened to the music, lost in their independent thoughts.

After awhile, the low buzz of conversation gradually

resumed, with occasional friendly banter across the bar from friend to friend.

"Well, Frankie, I notice you finally got excused by the wife for a minute or two!"

"Speak for yerself, John, I saw your woman walking up the hill lookin' for ye...better hide or she'll drag you back home to fixin' that door in two seconds!"

"Harry, me boy, I hear ye're startin' a salmon fishin' guide business in the spring at your little place on the Owenglin...need a hand, my friend?"

"Not at the moment, but I'll be lookin' ye up in two months or thereabouts."

The pub got busier, and a lively group of young people filed through the door, laughing and filling the room with noise and energy. "Let's hear something we can dance to!" someone shouted. The musicians obliged. The violinist nodded to his partners and smoothly shifted the pace from a melancholy tune into a lively jig. Soon the place was vibrating with motion and singing and raucous fun. Electric excitement permeated the room. Caught up in the spirit of it, Thomas clasped Maggie's hand and jumped up. "Dance with me, Maggie!" He nearly yanked her out of her chair and to the floor, and the pair joined in the merriment, swinging and circling and flying around among a rowdy mess of arms and legs and flushed faces.

Thomas hadn't danced with such total abandon in years, not since his college days. His mind was filled with the flashing colorful images of the other couples on the floor. He saw flickers of reds and oranges but couldn't remember seeing all those colors on people before the dance. There was something exotic and primitive about their movement. It made him feel alive and powerful. He knew that Maggie was there with him on the dance floor, but together they were miles and light-years away from the crowd.

From the happy smile on her face he knew she too was feeling the same magical transformation. She was his partner here and now and also in the past and in the future. The music peaked and soared as the musicians played faster, stomping their feet and challenging the crowd to keep up with them, until they came to a crashing, magnificent, climactic conclusion, and the crowd exploded with cheers and applause.

Draws of Guinness were readily slammed onto the table before the musicians, who thankfully downed their stout, nodded to each other, and then began to play a soft melody. Before two measures were played, a young woman wearing an apron and wiping her hands with a dish towel sat down beside the violinist, her clear, sweet soprano voice crooning a song. Several couples returned to their tables to cool off and quench their thirst. Others embraced and began to dance again, not ready to relinquish the dance floor but thankful for the slower tune.

Thomas had removed his sweater, threw it to his chair, and wiped his sweaty brow. Small patches of dampness darkened his shirt, and his face was flushed with the exertion and exhilaration of the jig. He was in good spirits, looking thoroughly happy. He looked at Maggie with a question, and she silently assented, raising her arms again to meet his. Tense at first, her stiffened back and limbs soon relaxed to the soothing sensuousness of the singer's voice, and she waltzed gracefully to Thomas' lead. Together they moved in small steps around the floor among the other dancers. Thomas felt Maggie growing more at ease in his arms. Despite the sweat he could still feel on his forehead, he held her closer to him.

She didn't mind the closeness at all. No, more than that, she welcomed it — the golden glow of the peat fire, the captivating music, the dimly lit coziness of the room, surrounded by couples in love (or at least, she reflected cynically, in love with the moment). She closed her eyes and let herself glide with him, swaying to the music. She set her mind free, allowed it to wander wherever it would; and when she did this, her mind became a conduit for the physical joy she experienced in this dance...the gentle firmness of his big, warm hand clasping hers, the slight pressure he placed on the small of her back to guide her, the occasional bumping of boot against boot as they turned about the floor.

Dreamily, she opened her eyes and looked up enough to see his neck fill her vision, almost touching her forehead. A drop of sweat slowly trickled from a lock of hair behind his ear down his neck; absent-mindedly, with her fingertip she caught the drop before it reached his collar, then stared with fascination at the glistening wetness. An impulse to reach up and lightly kiss his ear overwhelmed her, barely controlled by her long-conditioned reserve.

Now the pub was crowded and the little space of floor was expanded as patrons pushed tables back to make room for more dancers. Soon that space too was filled and the floor disappeared beneath the wave of partners. Thomas led her around the floor, the two of them gliding fluidly as a singular moving figure, and their motions blended as they learned the feel of each other's touch.

As they neared a dark corner a man and his partner bumped into them. Maggie was pushed into Thomas, caught off-balance, and he gripped her tightly. Her head banged lightly against his shoulder, and as she regained her balance her hip brushed against his; a heated blush washing across her face and neck in her awkwardness. They laughed together when another slight collision on the packed floor caught them by surprise, and he stabilized them both by pulling her close to him, her body clinging intimately to his. Her womanly softness molded to his firm body. With a calm she didn't feel, Maggie pulled away gently and then, feigning a clumsy misstep, again closed the gap between them. In that instant a thousand sensations flashed in every nerve of her body.

They hesitated, and this time when they resumed their dance, swaying in unison, she didn't pull away. His palm flattened behind her, guiding her, and his fingers caressed her spine; and as he did this, she slipped her finger over his collar and onto his neck, stroking his damp skin, toying with the edges of his hair. From head to toe their bodies clung like magnets as the music guided the rhythm of their movement. The thrill of her touch rushed through his veins. Likewise, Maggie knew equally exquisite pleasure in his touch.

The violin and the singer's voice brought the music to a low, poignant end. Lost in the midst of the crowd, Maggie and Thomas lingered in their embrace, reluctant to let the magic fade. In the faint, golden orange glow of the firelight they stood for a moment, looking steadily, deeply into one another, willing each to know what they wanted to say. Unable to say it out loud, she slowly dropped her arms from around his neck and looked downward, as if examining her hiking boots had suddenly become a consuming concern.

"Hey, Americans, in this country when the music stops, that's a clue the dance is over," the drummer called across the room to them mischievously, "but don't let me stop you!" and he tapped a light thump on his drum. The crowd laughed, Maggie and Thomas joining them and wondering how easily these Irish detected Americans in a crowd.

Then, flustered by the stimulation of moments just passed, Maggie mumbled, "Time to go...I'm afraid that Irish coffee made me woozy." She picked up her shopping bags and jacket and hurried toward the door. "I want to make sure Eamon got here all right."

Thomas caught up with Maggie outside and she slowed her pace. Silently, with the muffled noises of the pub receding and the brightness of a street lamp lighting their way, he walked her back to the Clifden Arms. In the solitude of the hallway between their rooms, he held up his palm toward her. She held hers up to his, and with complete understanding they touched again, hand against hand, fingers tip to tip, saying nothing, nothing needing to be said. She turned and went into her room. He lingered for a moment, looking absently at the closed door, the emotions of the night filling every crevice of his head and heart and body.

* * * * * *

The cold whoosh of the ocean waves on the shore couldn't dull Thomas's exhilaration when he and Maggie set out in the morning, with Eamon following closely behind. Thomas smiled thoughtfully. He had a good intuition about the device, he had Maggie's almost undivided attention, and for the first time ever, he felt sure about his feelings for another human being. He loved her. His confidence soared earlier when he logged onto his Internet service and found a message from her far down on the list of incoming mail, which he skimmed as he quickly downed a cup of tea and dressed to meet the two journalists for breakfast. When he got to Maggie's note, he was disappointed in its brevity but encouraged by the message. *Thanks, Fred,* it read, *I had a lovely evening. Next time you can lead. Ginger.* He grinned and jotted a quick reply. *Ginger? I thought you were Lesley.*

Up the coast they turned onto a rutted road outside Renvyle. Far out on a point Maggie pointed to the ruins of a castle at the top of a bluff overlooking the ocean. Eamon honked and waved them toward the tall tower surrounded by crumbling stone. He wanted to stop to film it, and the forbidding slope of the hill wouldn't deter him. He zoomed around them and began to climb the hill.

Thomas followed him, pushing the little four-cylinder car's engine up the steep, slippery path, but the tires weren't designed to grip ice, and the car slid sideways until they stopped perilously close to the edge of the road and the sharp drop to the ocean. He spun the wheels, trying to rock the car, but it wouldn't move. The smell of burning rubber on the ice and gravel warned him to give up.

"I'll push," Maggie started to get out of the car, but he stopped her and jumped out first.

"No, you drive, I'll push." She climbed across the emergency brake into the driver's seat and honked the horn to alert Eamon. As Thomas crouched and leaned his shoulder into the back end, Eamon came slipping and sliding down the hill on foot and joined him. After three attempts, they finally rocked it out, stumbling to their knees as the car lurched forward. Maggie let it roll a few feet down the hill, looked in the rearview mirror, and threw the gear into reverse, backing up the hill, over the icy patches and past the startled men. She stepped on the brake, pulled the emergency brake, and climbed out, grinning triumphantly.

"Now then, anyone want to inspect some ruins?"

The view from the top of the tower was spectacular. The wind snapped around them, stinging their eyes, forcing them to clutch their jackets closed. The magnificent power of the blackish sea swelling and cresting, then crashing white waves high over the rocks held them spellbound. Eamon almost forgot to film it until Thomas said something.

"Here, let me take a picture of you two," he stepped back a few paces to the far wall of the tower and focused on Maggie and Eamon, silhouetted by the tower window and the bluish violet of the skies beyond it. Maggie nestled her arm through Eamon's, smiling up at him while Eamon hammed it up with a haughty, aristocratic mug. Through the lens of the camera, Thomas noticed something that hadn't been obvious to him before...Maggie and Eamon were companions, confidantes...and a twinge of jealousy nipped at him as he snapped the camera and the shutter clicked.

Deferring to Maggie's driving skills, Thomas climbed into the passenger seat. Soon they had left Renvyle behind and followed the winding road across a sweeping landscape of golden brown and auburn rolling plains and crystallized lakes cupped between the snowcapped Connemara Mountains, around windswept beaches and bluffs, past resort areas buttoned up against an unusually cold winter day.

Everywhere sheep wandered in flocks occasionally infiltrated by black rams, whose wool was as dark as the peat mounds in the bogs flanking their rock-strewn meadows. Several times the cars swerved as they avoided collisions with the woolly beasts standing stupidly on the road, bleating in protest at the honking cars and lazily scattering on either side. Hibernating farms with antiquated machinery beside old sheds lay dormant for the winter. Several times they stopped at Eamon's signal to take pictures and to videotape the vast open hills and the sweeping peat bogs.

At Maam Cross they stopped for lunch.

"Thomas, what do you say I ride with Eamon awhile so we can go over some of our notes?"

"Fine, but we might want to get into Oughterard soon...see those dark clouds rolling in?"

"Aye, let's not waste any time. I want to get some footage of Aughnanure Castle before we call it a day." Eamon wolfed down his sandwich and went out to the phone booth to make a call.

"Why do you suppose he makes so many phone calls?" Thomas watched after him.

Maggie flippantly suggested, "I don't know...according to him, he's got a lot of girl friends tearing their hearts out for him. He's probably got a bookie, or maybe he checks in with his mother every day." She stopped short when she noticed Thomas's concerned frown.

"Thomas, what are you thinking?" He didn't answer. She leaned close to him and stared until he looked her in her eyes. "I trust him, Thomas."

"Okay, yeah, you're right." However, Thomas took the seemingly unrelated tidbit of information and filed it in his head. It was a loose piece that didn't quite fit. Thomas remembered the jigsaw puzzles he did as a kid and recalled that if he didn't think about the individual pieces, sometimes they fell into place. Changing his approach, the particular piece he turned over in his fingers would suddenly fit in with all the others and as if by magic the picture would become clear.

His desk at work was structured like that, although no one recognized it. It was arranged like a giant puzzle with thousands of many-sided pieces that only Thomas could suddenly bring together in a brilliant creative flash. Of course looking at his scribbles and notes and pieces of unattached paper, no one would expect that there was a real system to the way he left his desk.

Anyway, he didn't feel threatened by Eamon, and he trusted him, yet he wished he knew more about him.

The skies had turned a whitish gray as they parked their cars in an empty lot outside the castle grounds. They walked down a boardwalk along a creek-sized river overgrown with moss-covered trees and dripping with ivy. In a small cottage nearly concealed within the woods, they found the groundskeeper, who was surprised by the appearance of visitors at this time of year. However, he loaned them the key to the gate and directed them up a path to its entrance.

A thousand voices from seven hundred years of generations seemed to whisper in their ears as the trio trudged across a short but massive bridge and pulled open the heavy doors of the castle gate. Once inside the courtyard they separated, each one exploring the grounds, peeking through arched doorways that led from the interior grounds to a pasture and woods, climbing moss-coated stone steps and walking the stone-walled perimeter, making their independent discoveries.

Eamon circled the main building — a twenty-five foot square tower six stories high — and mounted its winding stairway to the top. From his perch he could see Lough Corrib, rimmed with tree-covered islands, and directly below him he could gaze, unnoticed, at Maggie.

She was leaning against the stone of an arched doorway ten meters from the tower base, her eyes closed, a slight smile turning up the corners of her mouth. She must have thought she was alone and quite unseen, because she seemed to be lost in her own world, daydreaming. Slowly her hand lifted to her hair and her fingers combed through the curls, almost as if she were imagining it to be someone else playing with her hair; then she hugged herself and half-smiled again.

Around a corner of the arch Thomas appeared, startled by Maggie's presence. She was startled, too, and for a second they stood breathless and then laughed. Eamon continued to watch from his vantage point above them as Thomas took Maggie's hand and led her to a high stone wall next to the arch and leaned back against it, pulling her close. The air had developed a thick mist, turning into a fine drizzle, and Eamon had to blink the water from his lashes to see as Thomas took Maggie in his arms, hugged her, and then, as she lifted her face to his, kissed her deeply.

The aching in Eamon lay like an anvil upon his chest, and he backed into the dank dinginess of the tower so he wouldn't be caught eavesdropping, pining for what he knew they shared.

* * * * * *

Outskirts of Oughterard, near Lough Corrib

"Maggie, look there for a second," Thomas nodded toward a car parked on the edge of the road as they passed it. "I've seen that guy before, at least a couple of times." There was something peculiar about the man's stance. He was bent stiffly over the open hood as if to check the engine, but his head was turned toward them and he looked hard at the Opal as if studying its occupants. Watching the man from the rearview mirror, Thomas glimpsed a patch of red hair under a black cap.

"Yup, I know I've seen him before."

"Where?"

"I can't remember."

Maggie, back in the passenger seat, glanced in the side view mirror. "Oh, Thomas, he's probably an industrial spy keeping track of our movements," she quipped, opening her eyes wide, teasing him, dismissing his concern. She squeezed his arm, trying to lighten him up. Unwittingly she had voiced exactly what he was seriously considering. He smiled, but when Maggie looked away, he took another look in the rearview mirror.

Changing the subject, he said, "Read the directions to the B and B again, will you?"

Bridgid, a sturdy, blond-haired English woman with ruddy cheeks and a loud voice, opened the door to the tall man standing on the stoop of the bed and breakfast in the sleet, his auburn hair and brows flecked with ice, his hands pink with wet and cold.

"Oh my, you must be the gent who called! I'm so delighted to see ye. Thank the Lord you made it through this dreadful storm! Tilde, get down! Stop sniffin' the gent, it's not polite...bad dog! Please come in, I've got yere rooms ready for ye! Good thing you arrived now, it's lookin' like a desperate storm out there tonight! Oh, and them's must be your companions waiting in those cars out there? Bring them in, then!"

Bridgid pushed Tilde, an overgrown Golden Labrador, away from the door and pulled it open. The three wet visitors scurried in from the courtyard parking lot with their bags as the wet sleet thickened and poured around them.

The fiftyish, well-endowed woman helped them remove their jackets and shook off the icy drops. Ever curious about her guests, she gave each of them the once-over, her cheeks becoming flushed as she gave extra time to inspecting the tall, handsome physique of Eamon from the ground up. He winked at her when her curious gaze reached his eyes, and she became flustered.

"Ah, boyo, I can see you're full o' the devil terrible!"

"Aye, woman, and you'd better watch out, because me cousin might be coming right behind, and he's twice the devil of me!" He grinned at her wide-eyed stare, and when she finally broke a wide smile, a high-pitched giggle escaped from her bountiful chest and she turned to lead them down a long hall past a tiny kitchen to the back of the house.

Here a group of bedrooms and a central bathroom led off from a spacious round hall. Bridgid swung open each of the doors with a flourish as if unveiling a grand ballroom, letting rosy light flood the hallway from each direction. Looking for and finding the pleased expressions on her guests' faces, she directed the men into their rooms and said she'd be along in a wee moment to make sure they were settled in comfortably.

She followed Maggie into her room, a compact, cozy box decorated with a decidedly feminine, flowery influence — old-fashioned rose wallpaper, pink lamps on the walls, thick deep rose carpet, a dainty white vanity and closet, and a lace covered fluffy bed that dominated the room.

"Will this do then? I'll have some tea ready in a moment, and I'm stoking the fireplace in the parlor just now. The bed has an electric blanket on it. I'll be getting central heating in another year, don't you s'pose these winters are frightfully cold?"

"It's lovely, thank you. I'm exhausted...think I'll get out of these dripping clothes and rest a bit."

"Very good, dearie. The bathroom's right around the corner and there's plenty of hot water for a good soak. If you need anything 'tall, I'll be watching me soaps in the kitchen." Bridgid started to close the door, then looked back at Maggie, turned and peeked out the door, and leaned in, signaling Maggie to come closer.

"Miss," she whispered, "The tall one...he's a bit cute to be so desperate for a woman's company, ain't he?"

"Aye," Maggie looked at her with a pseudo-serious expression and whispered back, "He's mighty sweet but a bit lacking in the charm department. He's forgotten how to talk to ladies after being away in the penitentiary so long, and getting powerfully lonely. We're watching him closely, Bridgid...never fear, if he starts to get too forward with you, you just let me know straightaway, all right?"

"What'd he do, ma'am, to be locked away?"

"I haven't got the actual story out of him yet, Bridgid, but I gather it had something to do with a horrendous fight, defending the reputation of a lady, that ended with a mortal blow. At least, I think that's the way it went."

Bridgid drank in Maggie's suppositions with fervor, open eyes and a rounded mouth, raising her hand up to her mouth to stifle a shocked "Oh!" while she nodded slowly and backed out of the room. Excited she was to have under her roof a stranger whom she elevated to the position of convicted murderer with a chivalrous story behind his crime. She couldn't wait to tell Frannie next door.

"A courageous girl, you are, traveling about with him...be careful, dearie," she whispered, placing grand emphasis on her last phrase, and looked carefully into the hall before stepping quietly away and closing the door with a faint shush.

Maggie nodded and smiled as the door closed and she heard Bridgid knock on the other doors, asking in a hushed tone after the men's comfort, lingering at Eamon's door, and asking could she see to anything for them? Maggie heard the innkeeper's footsteps recede down the hall as she looked about the room for electrical outlets, kicked off her boots, and started to organize her things, unzipping her computer bag to remove her laptop and cables. Moments later she heard a soft tap on her door.

"Could you just leave the tea out there, Bridgid, please?"

"It's not Bridgid."

She leaned her cheek against the door, closed her eyes, and felt her heart pound.

"Maggie, it's me...may I come in?"

She opened the door wide enough for Thomas to enter and quickly closed it again. He had already removed his wet jacket and changed into dry clothes. His wet hair had been combed, and he was holding a tray of tea and two cups. She couldn't help smiling when she noticed wedges of a Tobler orange chocolate on one of the saucers. From his back pocket he pulled a flask of brandy and poured some of the amber liquid into the cups, followed by black tea.

"You're still wet and cold. Here...I intercepted Bridgid. This might help."

Maggie didn't answer; she just nodded half-wittedly, watching him, warmed by his presence. He leaned over her and kissed her gently on her forehead, then paused and kissed away the raindrops still lingering on her brow. She stood still, dumb and happy, watching him as he unbuttoned her jacket and slipped it off her arms. It smelled of wet wool. He set it on a chair near the radiator to dry. He smelled clean, like soap, and Maggie thought he must have settled in his room awfully fast before coming across the hallway. She shivered. He lifted a cup of tea and brandy to her lips, and she let him help her drink it. Then he held the Tobler wedge up to her mouth and she bit off a corner of it. She closed her eyes and waited.

Watching her, he embraced her tenderly and held her still, transferring warmth from his body and extracting the chill from hers. When he felt her relax and snuggle into him, he tucked his hand under her chin and lifted it. She opened her eyes and looked at him and, except for a barely perceptible nod, didn't move. He reached for the bottom of her sweater and pulled it over her head.

Again she closed her eyes, standing very still, unusually calmed by the touch of his big, warm hands against her undershirt, holding her bared shoulders, his thumbs tracing circles on her neck as he kissed the top of her head. She felt him studying her face while he removed her undershirt, then her jeans, kneeling down and supporting her as she stepped out of each leg. He stood again, hugged her, kissed her brow and then gently, as if she might break, kissed her lips. Tasting a trace of orange-kissed chocolate, he licked the corner of her mouth with the tip of his tongue, then touched her lips with his again.

She opened her eyes.

"What about Eamon?"

"Shhhh. Don't worry about Eamon. He's busy in the kitchen, charming Bridgid out of some whiskey. She's filling him in on the soap operas, no doubt." He smiled.

She closed her eyes and relaxed, relinquishing control. Guiding her with his hands, he backed her to the bed and sat her down upon it. She felt the mattress shift as he sat down next to her. He rubbed warmth up and down her arms, then leaned over and pulled off her socks. He lifted her legs onto his lap and massaged her still icy feet one by one, kneading circulation into the toes and the tops and the arches, occasionally caressing her calves and leaning down to plant a kiss on each of her knees.

When she was warm and no longer shivering, he pulled back the bedclothes and laid Maggie's head back onto the pillow. Unseeing, she climbed under the covers and lay still, allowing his hands to move about her body, removing her undergarments.

The mattress shifted again, and she wondered what was happening, where he was. She tried to visualize what she might see if she opened her eyes, yet she kept them closed. She listened to the muffled sounds of his movements. She felt feverish, moist flashes across her body...between her breasts, below her ears, in the crooks of her elbows.

Then it was completely quiet, no sounds to give her a clue about what was happening outside her closed eyelids. He waited patiently until finally, slowly, she opened her eyes and looked at him. She watched him with clear, sparkling eyes, sure of him, sure of herself.

"Come here, Thomas." She pulled back the blankets. He stood over the bed for a few moments, appreciating her, willing them to take it slowly. Deliberately, he sat on the bed and leaned over her, balancing on one elbow as his other arm reached up to her hair. With every ounce of self-control he could muster, he avoided touching her body and focused instead on her face, tracing the outline of her cheekbones, over her brow, down her temple, around her jaw to her upper lip; and his finger settled there. She opened her mouth, reached for his fingertip, then closed her mouth around it, feeling the ridges of his fingerprint, tasting his clean skin, staring into his eyes, smiling with silent joy.

He pulled his finger from her mouth, pressing it softly against her breast. Instantly she responded. He kissed her lips again, then her chin, sucked gently at her throat, then traced a path with agonizing slowness across her breasts. Her senses unleashed, she pulled him to her ardently, and when he knelt above her, they wrapped themselves around each other and led their joint passion to a heady, electrifying release.

In the black of the night, sleet spattered against the window, making gritty tapping sounds until two o'clock in the morning, when clouds warmed the night air enough to turn the sleet into a slushy drizzle for another hour. Finally it ceased. From the kitchen of the bed and breakfast, a radio playing big band music had replaced the drone of television soap operas. The muffled sounds of giddy laughter filled the silence between songs.

And in the room at the very back of the house, the lovers let their passion command their actions as they brought each other to fiery physical heights again and then fell, entwined in each other's arms, exhausted, into a heavy, dreamless slumber.

chapter 9

CHRISTMAS IN CAVAN

A soft grayness illuminated the morning skies and seeped through the windows around the quaint Irish house. Thomas and Maggie teased and wrestled their way down the hall to the dining room off the parlor. They pulled their chairs up to a neatly laid table of linen napkins, fine china, and heavy silver surrounded by glasses of orange juice, a pot of tea, marmalade, hard butter, and toast racks. A cluster of candles burned in the middle of the small table, flickering in a dancing duet with the flame in the fireplace.

Maggie poured tea for Thomas and herself.

"Do you know how to make a proper cup of tea?"

"Who, me? Back home, I'd never think of drinking tea."

"Really? Well, there's only one way to prepare tea correctly, Thomas."

"Is that right? Tell me, Miss O'Connor."

"Well, it's simple really. First you put the water on to boil. Place your tea in your pot, and when the water's boiling rapidly, pour it over the tea. Now, if you want, you can add honey — sugar if you don't have honey — but never,

ever put artificial sweetener in the pot before you add the boiling water...you'll just make a mess."

"Oh, well now you've hit on something I'm good at. Messy I can do."

"Sheez."

As if on cue, Bridgid entered with two plates of eggs and bacon. Was it instinct, Maggie wondered, that signaled these innkeepers that their guests were up and about? Were their ears tuned in to every little household noise? The thought made her blush.

"Well then, ye slept well, did ya?" She looked from Thomas to Maggie and seeing the color on Maggie's face, the amusement in Thomas's eyes, she maintained a diplomatic, demure countenance and set their plates before them.

Eamon entered the room just then, stretching. "Like a wee babe, Bridgid, my love! And ravenous! Bring me victuals, my glorious vixen!"

"Oh my, oh me boyo, right away then!" Off she hurried for another plate, unaware of Maggie's chuckle and Eamon's amusement at her flustered departure. Meanwhile, Eamon looked about for a chair and sat at another small table next to Maggie.

"Ready to head back toward Cavan, love? Halfway across country at Athlone we turn north, but before we do, I'd like to take you to Clonmacnoise and show you a special turn of the River Shannon. It's a place not ever to be forgotten once you've been there, so it is."

Bridgid re-entered with Eamon's breakfast. "Aye, lass, you must go there, and tread the very stones that the Pope himself did when he prayed at Clonmacnoise in the nineteen hundred and seventies." She sat down in the chair across from Eamon and recounted, as if she were not a storyteller but a sixth century missionary who'd been there, the legend of St. Ciaran, who initiated the construction of a great monastery on the Shannon River.

"Many kings were buried there, includin' your O'Connor ancestors Turlough and Rory, who was himself the last high king of our Erin. Oh darlin', ye must be figurin' to visit the grand O'Connor ancestral home in Castlerea?"

"I hadn't given it much thought...you mean there's actually a house and not a ruins?"

"Aye, dear, though this one is more contemporary...1880, I believe it was built."

Maggie hesitated. "I don't know, Bridgid, I've wanted to learn more, but don't know that there's enough time. I didn't plan to do any historical research on this trip, and anyway, there are so many living, breathing people to learn about, I think I'll concentrate on them."

"Well, at least when you get to the monastery, say a prayer for your family and look for an O'Connor grave or two. Now eat your breakfast, dear, before it gets cold."

"I've got to check messages before we leave," Thomas said as he scooped a forkful of eggs into his mouth.

"One phone...me first! I have to leave a check-in message with George, and I want to call Paddy and Ceil in Belturbet to let them know they'll be having an additional guest for Christmas."

Belturbet, County Cavan...Paddy...coincidence? With raised brow, Thomas looked first at Maggie, then at Eamon.

"This bed and breakfast in Belturbet you told me about...it wouldn't be a fishing resort, would it?"

"Yes, it is! Paddy is a fishing guide...wait till you hear some of his..."

"I believe we have a mutual acquaintance here, Maggie." Thomas looked at his watch. "Excuse me, I do need to leave some instructions on Matt's voice-mail so he'll get it right away when he gets to the office." Eamon and Maggie looked at him questioningly, but he offered no explanation.

* * * * * *

Pulling up to Stag Hall, with Eamon jerking to a stop in the other car behind him, Thomas braked the Opal and turned off the ignition. A man came from around the back of the house carrying a load of peat...was this the Paddy who had arranged his meeting with Dr. Pennton?

"Welcome back, Maggie girl," Paddy said with a big smile, approaching the car. "Ho, Eamon, my boy, you're back here too...this is grand! And another guest we have here then?" No mistaking his voice...this was the man Thomas had talked with by phone a few days ago. Paddy extended a hand to him as Thomas got out of the car, and Thomas shook it with a firm grip, smiling and looking directly into Paddy's eyes.

"Hello, Mr. Brennan. I'm Thomas deFremond."

Paddy stopped in mid-shake, briefly, looked carefully into Thomas's eyes, then smiled broadly in recognition and continued shaking his hand enthusiastically.

"deFremond, you say? Well, well, this is a grand day. I'm glad you're here, son. Welcome to my home." More quietly, in a hushed tone meant for Thomas alone, he added, "Ian's told me about your visit...I want to help in any way I can."

Bewildered, Maggie looked at Thomas for explanation.

"Later, okay?" he asked, and she nodded. "Let's get our things in and get settled first."

* * * * * *

An hour later, Paddy joined Thomas and Maggie in the parlor, sitting in his big worn chair by the fireplace and lighting up a cigarette, repeating the same movements he'd made thousands of times since that chair had been set by that fireplace thirty-two years before.

Paddy glanced at Maggie. Thomas answered his silent question with a nod...she could be trusted. Paddy smiled in assent, and asked, "Well, Thomas, what's your take on the device?" Thomas sat forward, excitement shining in his eyes.

"Paddy, what Ian showed me...it works. It could be a breakthrough that establishes a role for Ireland as a worldwide technological player. The part that I don't follow is why some company here hasn't jumped on his idea and run with it. Here's this method of sandwiching glass sheets together to create the entire monitor, no CRT tube, few electronics and at a potentially insignificant cost to produce."

"It's one of those discoveries that just happened when he was researching something else for one of the glass companies," Paddy continued for Thomas. "He approached a company in Dublin and they turned him down. That's why he's back in Cavan. The crystal factory was very interested as soon as he called on them, and now they're planning to work together. Since this isn't a typical thing for a crystal shop, nobody will suspect until we're ready to go to production. The owners are quite an innovative lot."

Thomas leaned forward. "If production of the screen can be funded by an Irish firm, it could conceivably boost Ireland's economy. On the other hand, if an American company funds the project, it could get very complicated politically, particularly if a British-owned company like mine gets into it. What's your connection with John Walker?"

"Aye, him." Paddy scowled. "He came here for a week of fishin' last summer and overheard me and Ian discussin' Ian's work. He got interested and hasn't stopped pesterin' me since. I've made no commitments to him, nor has Ian."

"I have an eerie feeling about this." Thomas looked worried, a prickly memory crossing his conscience.

"What do you mean?" Maggie asked. Paddy and Thomas looked at each other.

"I don't know...it takes me back to something else that happened to me many years ago, when I was in graduate school. I was unwittingly on the peripheral of a drug deal. The bad guys, the ones who I *think* were the bad guys were all buddy-buddy with the ones I thought were the good guys. It's a very long story. One day a girl I knew from the apartment house where I lived asked me to take her to the Federal Courthouse. She was being questioned by the feds about a drug deal her ex-boss was somehow involved in. She was ratting on the group. I went with her and stayed outside waiting for her to give all she knew, which was a lot...the vessel it was coming in on, the method of concealment, the whole works. It was a multi-million dollar deal.

"Anyway, I watched her come out of the building with these guys and thought no more about it, figuring I had done my Boy Scout deed by supporting her decision to tell the feds...moral support. I was just a guy from her apartment that she would talk to occasionally over coffee. That was on a Tuesday. Wednesday night I was in a restaurant with a date when these same guys — I thought they were federal agents — came in and sat at the next table with the guys she was ratting on. I heard much of the conversation.

At first I thought they were working undercover, then it hit me they were all in on it together."

"What did you do?"

"I did nothing. I just learned that some things you think you have a handle on are a lot bigger than they seem."

Maggie watched Thomas as he spoke...he fidgeted and seemed nervous, a fearful look in his eyes. She was seeing something in Thomas that apparently her blind love had hidden before, the imperfect parts of his nature that contrasted with the flawless image she had constructed in her mind. On one hand, she could understand his fear in a situation like that, but on the other hand... She didn't want to judge him too harshly, but with typically high expectations, now she questioned his judgment. She frowned and asked in a tight voice, "What happened to your friend?"

"It doesn't really matter, Maggie. The point is, we may be getting ourselves into a situation that's much bigger than anything we can handle."

She didn't like his answer...it bespoke a cold detachment. "But what happened to her?" she insisted.

"I moved to L.A. and for awhile I was in touch with her through a friend. She was pretty wild, Maggie, I suspect she finally was done in."

"What do you mean, 'done in'?"

"Well," Thomas was becoming impatient with her insistence, "she either OD'd or the jerk she ran around with finally killed her."

Now she was worried, translating his story to the present situation. "Do you think the professor's in some kind of danger? Paddy, do you?"

"It's nothing to worry about, I'm sure, Maggie dear...we're just being cautious, you know." Paddy's softly spoken words proffered a second message: Enough said, best to keep quiet. She looked thoughtfully at Thomas, who was lost in long repressed, stinging memories. She could see that whatever he was thinking about agonized him. She wondered what he had left out of his story. Whatever it was, his face belied the stoicism he had tried to project a moment ago. She wanted to console him but knew instinctively that continually dredging up the past might prolong his pain. God knew her own past was painful enough without going on about it all the time.

"Where's Eamon?" she changed the subject. Thomas wondered where Eamon was, too, but Paddy answered right away.

"He's talking with Ceil at the moment. I gather he has a soft spot for her cookin' and he's tryin' to charm her out of a slice of home-baked bread."

Restless, Maggie got up and moved to the window, looking out at the blackness. Turning her gaze in the direction of the side yard, she saw big flakes of snow drifting through the light of a yard lamp perched high on a pole. Thickly the snow fell. She followed the path of one little cluster of flakes that fell against the window and slid down to the sill.

"Hey! Snow! We'll have a white Christmas!"

Paddy and Thomas joined her and looked out at the white flecks floating amidst the darkness.

"It's pretty, aye, but 'twon't last, never does here, lass, it'll be gone by mornin'."

They watched the snowfall for a few minutes, then returned to their comfortable, overstuffed chairs by the fire. The two Americans and the Irish country gentleman fell silent, their eyes turning to the brightly burning peat fire. Separately, each focused on private but mutual thoughts.

* * * * * *

Christmas morning arose bright and sunny, the crisp air silent except for the crunch of boots on frozen grass in the yard behind the house. Mother Nature disclaimed Paddy's pessimistic certainty of a green Christmas, much to the Americans' delight. A thick, cottony blanket of snow covered the ground, and the trees were heavily laden with a crystal frost that glistened in the morning sun.

Maggie opened the heavy curtain and peered out, stretching and shivering alternately. Hugging herself for warmth, she leaned over and kissed Thomas on the forehead. Her disappointment in him the evening before had blurred through the night and her feelings had once again softened with the warmth of his closeness.

He didn't wake up. She blew softly on his eyes...he twitched. She shifted and pressed her cheek against his, humming "Jingle Bells." No response. Sighing, she climbed out of the bed and went into the bathroom.

Steam billowed out of the bathroom into the cold bedroom when she opened the door after her shower. Thomas was sitting up in bed, a red and white "Santa" hat tipped sideways on his head, smiling at her sleepily. Maggie pulled her thick robe tighter about her, sprinted across the icy floor and flopped onto the bed into his arms. He kissed her long and tenderly, and when she opened her eyes, he grinned and nodded toward something behind her. She turned and saw another Santa hat sitting on the pillow next to her.

"No way, I'm not gonna wear that! You look goofy enough for both of us!"

"Maggie, Maggie, it's Christmas! Humor me. I'd like to see what you look like as an elf." He kissed her again.

"Okay, but I get to be Santa and you be the elf." As she

lifted the hat, something small and hard fell into her lap. "Hey!" she jumped with surprise. Catching her up in his arms, Thomas reached for the little box. He hugged her tightly, then loosening his hold, he reached with one hand and held the box close in front of her face. She looked up at him and back at the box.

"It won't open itself, Margaret Marie."

As Maggie lifted the lid off the box, Thomas held it above eye level so she couldn't see the contents. She pushed herself up and peered over the edge of the box. Tears filled her eyes. The Claddagh ring she'd admired in Clifden. She was speechless, but it didn't matter because if she could think of any words, they would have stuck in her throat anyway. Tears spilled from her violet eyes. Thomas stifled her incoherent murmurs with another kiss as he wiped her wet cheek. Tenderly he took the ring from her trembling hand and slipped it onto her finger.

"I love you, Maggie, my best friend. I want to be part of your life...always."

Maggie looked at him tenderly as she studied the ring and let the significance of his words sink in.

"Wow, Thomas...wow." She sighed and looked at him with the earnestness she felt. "This is fast. I need to think about this, not because I'm not sure how I feel, but...well, I want to make sure you're sure."

"I'm sure," he said.

"Sure?"

"Sure as I can possibly be."

She smiled. "Okay."

"Really?"

"Really." She donned the hat and climbed on top of him, sitting on his belly. "But for now," she drawled," this best friend has designs on her best friend, and her intentions are entirely wicked."

With that, she threw her head back, tossing her hair out of her eyes and gazing down at him with a sensual invitation he couldn't resist. He reached for the tie on her robe and expertly loosened the knot. He bent up to kiss her while she tugged at his shorts. Scrambling under the covers together, they explored each other hungrily, laughing and kissing, groping and squeezing, teasing and touching each other, giving pleasure in the effortless way of two lovers who instinctively know the right things to do.

* * * * * *

TO: LazyJane

FROM: EZWriter

SUBJECT: Merry Christmas!

Dear Jane and Charlie,

Here's wishing you the merriest, most peaceful Christmas. As for me, I'm in an incomparable place with remarkable people. Eamon and I are making great progress...he's wonderful...want you to meet him someday. I've received an extraordinary gift and I'll tell you about it later when I call. Much more importantly, I've met someone. Be happy for me...there's no one on earth like him. Love you, and Happy New Year!

Maggie

* * * * * *

Morning rose the day after Christmas with sunny skies and warming temperatures. The snow that had cooperated to make the Americans' Christmas a white holiday was rapidly ascending in a floating mist of evaporating steam that swirled over the roads and pastures.

"I'm going to hike into Belturbet this morning, have a look around...anyone want to join me?" Maggie announced at breakfast.

"Well now, Maggie dear," said Ceil, "that sounds like a fine idea, but today is Boxing Day, everything will be closed up tight as the strings on Paddy's fiddle."

"We could still take a look around, and if there's no one about, we could hop the bus into Cavan, couldn't we?"

"Aye, the bus will be running, to be sure, and there might be a little more activity in Cavan Town, being a city and all, but we take our holidays seriously, girl, so don't count on doing any shopping."

"I'll take a chance...who's game?" she looked at Thomas, who nodded with a mouthful of breakfast, and then looked at Eamon.

"You go ahead, I'm going to stay and help Paddy with chores," said Eamon.

"Okay, and before we leave, Ceil, let me help with dishes."

"Oh goodness, no, Maggie dear, you're our guest!"

"And guests should be indulged? Please let me help...I need to do something with my hands besides write."

"Alright, that would be lovely!"

In the kitchen, Ceil handed Maggie a towel and showed her the cupboards. Maggie urged Ceil to tell her more about the photographs in the parlour.

"Aye, well, most of the pictures are of our three girls and their families."

"What about the ones of you? Like the one in the dance costume."

"That? Ah, well, my ma and da always wanted me to be a professional Irish dancer...preserve the tradition. I still teach the dance to children and grownups alike. But what I really wanted to do was act. I would have done anything to be in the theater."

"Well, apparently you made it? Some of those pictures show you up on a stage during a production?"

"Local productions, aye, after I married Paddy and moved here. And that's been great fun. And then of course there was the wonderful time with Aidann Quinn and the rest of the cast of 'Playboys' when we all went over to Redhills for filmin' several days. What I would have given, though, to be on the stage in Dublin — or London!" Wistfully Ceil sighed, her thoughts far away from this country house in rural County Cavan.

Maggie understood. She had felt the same kind of longing for something more when she was teaching. Only Ceil had settled for a completely different lifestyle, and Maggie was doing exactly what she wanted.

"But you met Paddy and came here instead?"

"Aye. And as much as I still dream about acting, I wouldn't have done anything different. Paddy is my Clark Gable, my Cary Grant, my Humphrey Bogart." She smiled at Maggie, and Maggie smiled, too. *Rare*, she thought, *to see such contentment in the eyes of someone who has sacrificed her dreams.*

* * * * * *

Maggie's camera did overtime as she paused again and again to click picture after picture as they hiked along the main road to Cavan. Route N3 took them past Stag Hall Parish Church and cemetery with its crooked rows of headstones that seemed to be shifting as if the ghosts beneath were playing mischief with the protocol of the resting dead.

They passed on temptations to turn onto smaller, unmarked lanes, where thatched roofs dripped watery beads of melting snow and boughs of trees hung heavily over the road. They made faces at the cows and laughed when the lumbering animals nonchalantly watched them with bright brown eyes and chewing cuds. They stopped to gaze at the lakes dotting the countryside, a brilliant blue this morning. A swirling vapor of evaporating snow drifted lazily through sunrays here and there, and the light dampness felt like an occasional touch of a soft hand against Maggie's cheeks.

"This, Thomas...this is what I want people to see in the documentary. As much as Ireland's economic progress, people should see the timelessness of this place."

Thomas gazed at her, admiring her fresh appreciation of everything she saw. "Save a little bit of this just for us, will you? Someday we'll come back here, and I don't want it to be overrun with Americans who've seen your documentary!"

Belturbet, as Ceil predicted, was buttoned up tight; even the pub wasn't yet open. Maggie sat down on the bench in front of the pub, Belturbet's official bus stop.

"Can't be more than just a half hour wait, I suspect," Thomas said. "That'll give me a chance to check in with Matt. Do you mind?" he pointed to a phone booth across the street.

"Go ahead, I'll just look around." She watched him

cross the street and enter the booth, deposit some coins and begin to dial. She brought her camera out of its case, zeroed in closely and focused on him, then snapped a series of shots of his expressions. How he moves me with his way, she thought as she watched him through the lens, feeling a surge of emotion as she captured his features over and over on film.

He finished his call and stepped out of the phone booth, looked casually up and down the street, then at Maggie, smiling. He sauntered across to her as she continued to shoot one frame after another until he was so close her lens could frame only his midriff. She lifted the camera away from her nose and looked up at him, grinning.

"Maggie, darlin', might I have this dance?" he held his hand out to her. His feeble attempt to imitate the lilting Irish brogue made her laugh, and she followed suit.

"Are ye daft, boyo? I can't dance when there's no music, and besides, we're on a street in Belturbet, not a dance floor."

But her protests fell on deaf ears. "Don't be sensible. Dance with me." Devilishly he laughed at her, his arm extended, persistently waiting for her to give. It took only a second of silent coaxing. She embraced his spirit and stood facing him, only inches away. Her mouth twitched, a slight smile appeared acknowledging his victory, and she raised her hand up to his. Together they swayed in the silent morning sun, a waltz with a rhythm set by the chemistry of their connection. Gradually Thomas increased their circle of steps and occasionally dipped her gracefully, twirling her now and bringing her face close to his, the two of them captivated by the magic of the unheard music.

From the second-floor window of the flat above the pharmacy next to the pub, an observant little boy, not more than four years old with unruly dark hair and marmalade smeared across his chin, chewed his toast and peered curiously at the couple's antics. His eyes widened and he giggled when Thomas dipped Maggie, having never before seen such adult silliness on the streets of his little village. Catching their mood, he began to sway and dip, his imaginary princess apparently mindless of the sticky mess he was making of her hands.

The chugging of the Eirann bus coming up the steep bend in the middle of Belturbet brought an end to the waltz, and the pair gathered up their things to board as it pulled to a stop in front of the pub. A jiggle and a lurch, and the bus was bound east for Cavan, two passengers added to its load. Maggie covered Thomas's hand with hers, looked sideways at him, and sighed happily.

"Ya didn't tell me," she said, continuing her brogue, "what a pleasure it could be, ridin' public transit." Thomas turned to her, and his eyes bespoke his earnestness.

"Well, look at you. You didn't tell me what a pleasure it could be, with you...everything...with you."

chapter 10

RUINS

When you are old and gray and full of sleep,
And nodding by the fire, take down this book,
And slowly read, and dream of the soft look
Your eyes had once, and of their shadows deep;

How many loved your moments of glad grace,
And loved your beauty with love false or true;
But one man loved the pilgrim soul in you,
And loved the sorrows of your changing face.

And bending down beside the glowing bars
Murmur, a little sadly, how love fled
And paced upon the mountains overhead,
And hid his face amid a crowd of stars.

William Butler Yeats, 1865-1939 (Dublin)

Two days later the trio parted ways once again when Eamon sent Maggie and Thomas ahead and turned off the main road at the Hill of Tara to tape more footage of the landscape. He promised to catch up with them in Dublin after their meeting with Ian Pennton. Maggie yearned to join him on his trek to Tara...after Bridgid's coaxing, her interest in learning about her ancestral past had been freshly renewed. She wanted to touch the ground that nurtured her ancestors, smell the air, see the three hundred sixty degree perfect vista of Eire. Then she looked at Thomas and shelved her desire for a link with the past in favor of a more compelling connection with the present.

As they approached the vicinity of Trinity University, Thomas frowned, looking about the neighborhood. Something was in the air, and it felt wrong. Maggie sensed it, too.

"Maggie, check your map, will you...are we getting close? The pub should be somewhere around here."

"There," she pointed, "there it is, right there. How should I act? Does he know I'm with you? Would you rather I wait outside so you can talk with him alone?"

Thomas looked at her sideways, not really understanding what she meant. "Act? Act like we're close friends and you're interested in meeting an inventor as much as I am. Be yourself. He's not going to chase you away."

"Really, Thomas, won't he object to me sitting there while you talk about this secret device?"

"I doubt it. Paddy's probably already told him you know about it."

The pub was noisy with the animated chatter of local patrons. But this particular chatter filled the air with a tight, apprehensive signal much different than the light banter that usually bounced off the walls of village pubs. Thomas couldn't make out what the conversation was about, but again he tensed. Thomas and Maggie took a table near the door and ordered their ale. Looking around, Thomas saw no sign of Pennton. Minutes passed. He drummed his fingers anxiously. Maggie watched the door for someone matching Thomas's description of the professor, and she occasionally glanced about the room.

Finally, agitated, Thomas stood up. "Wait here...I'm going to phone Paddy to find out if he's heard from Pennton."

"Okay. Hurry." He looked at her, detecting the edge in her voice. "That guy's been eyeing me since we came in," she explained.

Thomas glanced across the pub and noted a man standing at the bar, boldly watching them. He looked vaguely familiar, but Thomas couldn't put his finger on why or how. His nerves heightened, Thomas headed for the wall phone in the alcove by the men's room.

Moments later he returned. His eyes swept the length of the bar and darted back and forth across the pub. The familiar-looking stranger was gone and someone else sat on the barstool where he'd been.

"Let's get out of here. I need fresh air."

Outside on the street, Thomas turned to Maggie and held onto her arms so tightly she hurt. He stared hard into her face, not speaking. She knew he wanted to tell her something, but the words were caught in his throat. She winced, and he loosened his grip. He found his voice.

"Maggie, listen to me. Paddy wasn't home. Ceil said he was on his way to Dublin and gave me a cell number where I finally reached him. There was an accident, some kind of explosion at Pennton's apartment house. Paddy hasn't been able to reach Pennton. He didn't have any details, but he's on his way there now. We're to meet him. Can you reach Eamon and tell him to get there as fast as possible? Tell him to bring a rental camcorder...not his, that's important. We need to get a recording of what's happened. I don't believe this was an accident."

"What do you mean? My god, Thomas!" She fumbled in her purse and found the number of the hotel where Eamon was to check in for them when he arrived from Tara. Thomas showed her to the phone booth and handed her some coins. She dialed, stunned and afraid, while he paced in front of her, watching the motion around them.

* * * * * *

A half hour later, Eamon showed up and found Paddy, Thomas and Maggie standing on the street outside the apartment five short blocks from Trinity.

They stared up at a window ringed with ugly, broad streaks of black. The street corner was blocked off with crime tape. Flashing lights on riot task force vans warned onlookers to stay back, and local Garda scanned the crowd. Two Garda directed traffic toward a detour route. In front of the apartment, a fire truck and hose blocked the entrance. A TV van was parked next to a barricade. Reporters stopped people, shoving microphones in front of them, searching for anyone who could offer bits of information that would help build their story for the half-five news. Eamon exchanged glances with Paddy, then looked at their frightened American companions and asked, "Did you find out what happened?"

"Eamon, thank God you're here. The professor's loft was blown up. We don't know a thing other than that."

"Maggie told me he didn't show for your meeting."

"Did you bring a camera?"

"Aye," Eamon replied, holding it up and showing Thomas the rental label. Eamon's experiences in Belfast with the RUC had taught him to use a rental if he didn't want to risk losing his. "What do you want taped?"

"Get everything on tape that you can, alright?"

The four of them walked around the block to enter from an alleyway. A blockade stopped them there too, but they got a better view of the section of the building where Pennton's apartment was located. The windows were gone. A ladder truck filled the alley, its hose running to the roof. A fireman at the top of the ladder was retrieving the deflated hose. Lights from the truck glared, flashing a chaotic tension that elevated the sensibilities of everyone watching. Looking around, Maggie spotted the stranger in the pub who had been watching them earlier. "Thomas! Look!" she pointed toward the man and turned to get Thomas' attention, but he was talking to Eamon and Paddy. She looked back at an empty space where the man had been standing. She skimmed the crowd, spotting no one recognizable...he had disappeared.

A local resident scrambled up to Eamon when he saw his camcorder.

"Are ye with the telly? Damn near blew up the entire block! My house is right over there. Misses and I heard a tremendous whump. Scared the bejeesus out of me. I thought the whole house was goin' to shake apart."

Eamon aimed his camera at the local. "What time was that?"

"Must've been half-two on the nose. Missus just put down her magazine to start our afternoon tea. Say, what television channel are ye with? I don't see which one it is on your camera...don't you typically have your station somewhere on your camera?"

Eamon ignored his questions, feigning preoccupation with his camera as he panned the area, then opened the case and switched tapes, putting the used one in his jacket pocket. "Have you been here since it happened?"

"Aye. Major blast. Most frightful thing that's happened here as I recall. The sirens and the lights have been flashing all along."

"Did you learn what happened then?"

"Well, I heard, mind you, from one of the authorities that someone was storing paint and old rags up there next to some chemicals, and it just blew all by itself. Likely story, I say."

"Hear if anyone got hurt?"

"Now Laddie, that's the dreadful part. I heard that the old man what lived up there might've been inside, may even have been killed. The police have got my statement. I think they asked everyone here to tell 'em what we seen. I told them I saw nothing but I did hear the blast. IRA for sure, I tell ye. Such a shame, to bring their Troubles down here to the Republic now. Appalling, it is."

Maggie was horrified by what he was telling them. She looked over at Paddy and Thomas...they, too, were badly shaken by this account.

"Wait a minute now," Eamon cautioned his companions, "he may be exaggerating. We don't know that Pennton was in there. Let's try to get closer."

Thomas held Eamon back as he started toward the building. "No let's just get out of here."

They stared at each other, unsure what to do, then silently agreeing. As they turned with Maggie to move away, a uniformed riot officer stopped them. "Hold it. No unauthorized filming allowed. That's our orders. I'll take the camera."

"Hey! I'm a press photographer, you can't confiscate my camera!"

Thomas took the camera from Eamon and handed it to the officer. "Just give it to him. You can pick it up at the station later. Don't make trouble, Eamon."

Eamon started to protest, but the officer said, "Leave it alone, Laddie...you can pick up your camera at the downtown main house later."

Eamon grumbled, "See that nothing happens to my video, that's press property."

As the Garda took the camera and walked away, Eamon patted his jacket pocket, and with a subtle nod Thomas told him he understood.

The trio joined Paddy, leading him back to his car and away from the noise. He looked a long moment at Thomas, then took him aside and whispered something. Thomas's expression changed suddenly, and he looked at Paddy, surprised. Maggie wished she knew what they were saying, but knew not to interrupt. The two men nodded to each other in agreement and walked over to one of the Garda. An animated discussion ensued, and Maggie could hear them explaining to the Garda that they were friends of Ian and Kathleen Pennton. Another moment of exchanges, and they returned to Maggie and Eamon.

"They won't let us see the body...they seem sure it's Pennton. Let's get out of here." He embraced Maggie quickly and she could feel him trembling. He held her away so she could see his eyes. He was alarmed, shaken badly.

"Maggie, can you drive Paddy's car? Paddy and Eamon and I need to sort this out. We'll follow you to Belturbet. When we're back there we can look at what Eamon got on video."

She nodded slowly.

"Will you be okay driving if we're right behind you?"

"Yes, okay. My god, Thomas," she uttered, shivering,

"How are we going to tell Kathleen?" The three men exchanged dour glances.

* * * * * *

The skies were darkening with a clarity that brightened the stars, and moonlight flooded the Penntons' white-blanketed yard. Kathleen looked out the window, seeing nothing, dazed. Maggie stood near her, wanting to hug her, console her, wishing she possessed the means to ease the older woman's sorrow.

A half hour earlier they had turned into the Penntons' driveway and saw Kathleen leaning out the door waving them to come in from the cold. Paddy and Eamon had hustled her into the parlour while Thomas and Maggie lagged behind outside to let the Irishmen break the news to her. It was then that Thomas filled her in on what he had learned.

"Maggie, I don't know much, but I think he must have realized he was in danger. He sent a messenger out to Paddy's place last night with a package. It had his notes and a prototype. He's got those with him now."

"Do you think he was murdered?"

"I don't know...it might have been an accident, but it looks suspicious. Maggie, promise me you won't do anything, go anywhere or talk to anybody without letting me know, okay? Until we know what happened..." he didn't finish, and Maggie didn't have to ask.

Eamon leaned out the door, motioning for them to come in, a somber look on his face.

"Paddy's with Kathleen in the kitchen. She can hardly speak, she's so distraught. She's making tea, says she needs to do something, he's trying to comfort her. I asked him to keep her in there a few minutes."

Eamon reached in his pocket and pulled out the video-tape he'd exchanged with a blank one just before the Garda confiscated his camera.

"Let's have a look, shall we?" They went into the parlour. Eamon turned on the television and video player, slid the videotape in, and hit the "Play" button.

They watched the chaotic scene play out again on tape, then backed it up and replayed it twice more before Maggie spotted the stranger from the pub. "Look, Thomas, there he is!"

"That could be the guy we saw on the road by Oughterard, but it's hard to tell." He backed the tape up again and watched the footage of the redheaded stranger once more. He recognized the man he'd seen before.

"That's him...that's him." He scrutinized the scene. "Eamon, what do those markings on the wall look like to you?"

"It looks like a professional bomb to me...that was no accident, Thomas, I'm sure of it. But I haven't a clue who might have done it. Looks typical of work done by Protestant activists or IRA, but that's not likely in Dublin. I'm certain it's been made to look that way. My guess is that bloke in the video was involved somehow, and he's working for someone who wants Pennton's device."

* * * * * *

Maggie stood in the back doorway of the Penntons' kitchen entryway and watched across the yard. Through the shed window, in the dim light of the lab the American, the young Ulster man, and the Republic Irishman huddled around the big wooden table examining the prototype.

In a quiet murmur, Paddy explained to them how he had plugged it into the computer and almost had it working. He spoke in an uncharacteristically monotone voice, as though the information were a recitation. And he talked as though the professor were still alive, somewhat as people do about the deceased at the luncheon after a funeral...*She loves those wee ribbon sandwiches*, and *Yes, I know the place, it's lovely, John and I go there often.*

"The professor has found a way to etch this special glass so when he grows the crystal on it, it conforms to the etched matrix. Then he sandwiches layers of the stuff together. Somehow all the crests and troughs of the different layers match up and there are no wires, only a little chip on the edge that turns it all on. You should hear him explain it...he says it sounds as if you were in the audience at the Grand Dublin Theater. There are no wires to the individual seat. But each person in each seat can hear each instrument separately. All the sounds originate from one place — the orchestra. The chip thing works like that...turns on each separate seat to the full spectrum. You have to see it working to believe it. And look here...it's no more than a centimeter thick."

"Are the details in here on how to construct it?" Thomas asked. "He showed me his notes. They were all handwritten."

"I don't know. So far all I've come across are his instructions on how to get it working. I kept them all together here with the prototype. I just kept it all together. When I heard about the explosion, I brought the parcel with me rather than leave it lay somewhere. They must be somewhere in here." He began to fumble through the box, then found several sheets of legal paper with the professor's hand-scrawled notes. He handed a page to Eamon, who skimmed it quickly, reading phrases here and there out loud.

"It says, *'In working on the new glass etching process, I've stumbled onto something else...deposited a thin film of a crystal and when sandwiched together and excited by an electrical impulse displays three-D color...the flat plates could be used to produce new flat screen monitors for all televisions and computers, replacing all cathode ray tube monitors...testing not only the process for etching, depositing and sandwiching but also the means of controlling the electronic pulse to any pinpoint on the screen...have almost perfected flat screen...This crystal process could create a non-polluting industry with massive market potential using raw materials found in Ireland...must talk with Paddy...glass...silica...sand...barium — also used in enemas...palladium oxide'.*"

Eamon looked up at Paddy and Thomas, who were rifling through the rest of the papers. Thomas picked one up and read it to them.

"Here, listen to this. I think this may be it: *'The crystal seeded in the center of the plate creates concentric waves over the entire surface. The next layer seeded just out of register with the first creates concentric nodes and the third layer provides the third element of color and the triggering mechanism to turn on each null point discretely from all others in whatever color, hue and intensity. Instead of Cartesian coordinates, it requires Euclidian geometry to trigger the concentric three-dimensional matrix sandwiched between the layers of the special glass. The triggering is a bit like a symphony played in a perfect acoustic hall. Each member of the audience hears each note distinctly without having a wire running to his loca-*

tion in the hall. The generator can be at one point, the stage, so to speak. Simple, cheap to produce and almost impossible to reverse engineer.'"

Thomas stopped reading and looked up. "Paddy, this screen is the professor's legacy. We have to safeguard it and make sure it makes it to production. How long do you think it'll take to get it working?"

"I don't know. But I don't think we'd best leave it here. Let's get it over to my place."

"Do you think that's a good idea?"

"Where else are we going to take it? If they know we've got it, it doesn't matter where we go with it. But for now I don't want Kathleen to have to deal with anymore than necessary. We can figure out later where to move it to safeguard it from them."

"Them? Who are you talking about, Paddy? Who knows about it?"

Paddy slowly shook his head and whispered, almost inaudibly, to himself more than the others, "Don't know, but I'll find out, that I will."

Maggie offered to stay the night with Kathleen, and Ceil arrived later, after the men returned to Stag Hall Inn and told her about the events of the day. That night, the three women grieved in the compassionate, delicate way that women do...consoling, comforting, holding hands, sharing tears.

Back at Stag Hall, the three men worked on the prototype throughout the night. By then their fear had been replaced with a feverish energy and adamant resolve to bring to fruition the gifted old professor's dream. They were grimly determined to make it come to life.

* * * * * *

They got the device working in the early morning hours. After they knew it operated reliably, they finalized their plan and then collapsed into their beds. But they slept fitfully, each in his haunted restlessness replaying the nightmare of the day before and anxious about what would be occurring in the next few days, worrying about how nothing must go wrong.

Thomas woke to the sound of the phone ringing at half-seven that morning. Thomas could hear Paddy mumbling in the kitchen but could make out none of his part of the conversation. The door to Stag Hall opened and closed quietly, and Thomas heard the grinding of Paddy's car as he started it and backed out of the yard. Thomas jumped up and ran to the door but was too late to catch him. There was nothing to do but wait for his return...if Maggie called, he had to be there for her.

An hour later, Maggie knocked softly on Thomas' bedroom door and slipped in. She had returned from Kathleen's to Stag Hall with Paddy.

"Thomas, you need to talk to Paddy. Something else has happened. When I woke up, I heard voices out in the yard at Kathleen's. It was Paddy talking to some guys. I couldn't hear what they were saying, but now he looks absolutely frayed."

Paddy knocked on the half-open door and waited a moment before stepping in and shutting it.

"Thomas, you must leave the country. Forget the professor and his wild invention. It doesn't exist."

"Paddy, what? What are you saying?"

"Kathleen had visitors first thing this morning. She called me, and I went over to talk to them. Oh, they were good. They asked me a lot of questions. They wanted to know if I had ever worked with the professor. At first I told them that he and I were old fishing chums and chums don't talk business and besides, I wasn't schooled like he was, so how could I have worked with him?"

"Who were they?"

"They acted like businessmen. They didn't look like thugs or anything like that. I'm positive they knew more than they let on. They spoke in hushed tones. At first I figured they were from an Irish company, so I'm afraid I might have spilled too much. My mistake, I'm sorry, Ian," he said, closing his eyes for a moment and addressing his departed friend. "But they seemed interested in backing up the device with Irish money and gave me the impression that Ian had named me as the middle man in the negotiations. Thomas, you understand, if an Irish company was interested that's the way I would go. Then they started to ask who had I talked to about this. I told them John Walker in London. I didn't mention you. No need to bring you into this."

He stopped for a moment, swallowing hard, then continued.

"Another thing, Thomas, there was a man who stayed behind in their car — their driver I reckon. I couldn't see him clearly enough to say for certain, but I think he was the man in the videotape." Paddy quickly rubbed the top of his head — he had recognized him from the hair. He hesitated again, this time by the uneasy look on Thomas' face. He took a deep breath and said, "You must forget this entirely. These crooks are bad news. You must leave Ireland immediately. Go home, boy, before it's too late."

"Paddy, did you tell them you had actually seen the prototype?

"I told them that I'd never seen it actually working."

Maggie watched anxiously as Thomas stared at Paddy, thinking intensely, various scenarios circling his dread of more tragedy to come.

* * * * * *

Belturbet was a tiny village, but its long line of black-clad, trudging mourners stretched over a hill in the funeral parade toward the small graveyard where Ian Pennton would be laid to rest. His widow was flanked by Maggie and Ceil at the head of the line behind Father Carroll. Cousins, their families and all the rest of the relations and friends followed. Paddy, Thomas, and Eamon brought up the rear, watchful for anybody acting strangely.

The gathering of mourners was a somber lot. There wasn't the kind of murmured comments among them about how it was a blessing, the deceased was getting on in years, and it was his time. No — this man had so much yet to give, had such vitality, and was so full of ideas. The news of his sudden, violent death had been a blow to everyone who knew him.

That afternoon, after the luncheon food had been eaten and Ian's remembrance had been toasted numerous times, after most of the friends and relatives had left, Maggie approached Eamon.

"I'm going out for awhile, Eamon. Will you stay with Kathleen and Ceil, keep them calm?"

"Maggie..."

"Eamon, just leave it alone. I need to talk with Thomas."

He looked at her tenderly. "I'll be here. Take care, pet."

She picked up the car keys and drove under the gray

skies along the winding, rutted road to Drumlane Abbey, following the directions on the scribbled note Thomas had left on the table next to her bed.

The gray-brown stone ruins of the roofless, crumbling abbey looked bleak against the drab sky and the steely coldness of the small lough beyond it, which was thinly rimmed with ice. Even the tufted grass, powdered by the ice-capped snow, couldn't now soften the hardness of the aged, crumbling walls in the abnormally harsh afternoon light.

Maggie found Thomas standing inside the abbey, staring through an opening toward the lake. He turned to look at her, and she stopped at the far end of the roofless edifice. Something in the expression on his face, as hard as the Romanesque carvings on the stone of the ruins, stopped her from approaching him. They stood face-to-face twenty feet apart, and then she realized she was seeing not cold callousness in his eyes but rather the frigid stare of solid fear.

"Maggie..." he stopped, unsure how to continue.

"Thomas?"

"I'm going back to the States." He spoke stiffly, with an abruptness she hadn't heard before.

"When? What about Pennton's invention? Aren't you going to stay and help Paddy and Eamon with his device?"

"No." That was all, he said, no more. Maggie didn't know what to say. Thomas looked different, he was acting differently...why was he being so terse with her? She understood his fear and she wanted to help him. She tried again.

"Well, me too...going home. My assignment's almost done. Just a few more days and Eamon and I can wrap it up. We can go back together."

"Maggie! Damn it, I'm trying to say goodbye."

"What? What do you mean? Thomas, you're acting weird. You're scaring me!"

"We can't....we have to split up." He shivered and looked away.

At first she didn't understand. After their closeness, what they'd been through, she didn't think they could not be together. She closed the space between them and held onto his arms, but she couldn't close the emotional distance his rigid stance conveyed.

"What? Hey, I know you're worried. So am I. But..."

"Stop it, Maggie."

"Stop it? Stop what? What happened to 'I want to share my life with you'? Are you saying now you're not in love with me?"

"I'm afraid it's far more complex than that. It's bigger than we are."

"More complex? Life is complex, don't you know that by now?"

He whirled around, flinging her arms off his, his back to her. He wanted to tell her so much. Instead he threw up his hands, looked at the sky and groaned, a low, guttural groan that emerged from deep within his being. He began to talk quickly, hammering the situation out before her.

"I can't deal with this anymore! Suddenly I have to make decisions that I can't handle. I've been warned to leave the country. You've seen what they can do...Pennton may not be the only one they were after! I don't trust my British boss. I think my American boss may be behind it. And Walker — who knows how he plays into this? This morning at the funeral I was approached by some guy who claims he's ex-CIA." Thomas whipped around and faced her, his eyes wild. "And you, Maggie...I fell in love with you online, on a computer, of all things!"

"Wait...calm down...think, Thomas. Think about the last few days. We aren't a cyber fantasy. I love you too, do you know that? God, Thomas! I'm the one who needs order and logic in my life, not you! You thrive on disruption and randomness. How do you think I feel about all this? We can get through this together."

He failed to find an answer that would satisfy her. But he tried.

"I care about you, Maggie, please know that. But I have to get away from this. I'm going to go back to New York, resign from Holmes, and try to find some normalcy somewhere, somehow. I'm going to forget about this invention and everything else about Ireland. And you should do the same. I'm scared, alright? Leave me alone!"

Disbelieving, she tried once more to hug him, tried to feel his warmth. Instead she felt only a cold, barren tower of arms and chest, his shoulders shrugging her off. In a voice as colorless as the December sky, he said, "We're over, done. This is it. I can't see you again. I need to get away."

She stared at him, shivering against the chill of his words, vaguely conscious of the hot tear that drew a red streak down her face.

Panicking, she wrung her hands. She felt the Claddagh ring and twisted it off her finger. She held it out to him, but he refused to take it. She reached out again and dropped it in his pocket.

"Keep this, Thomas. Remember what it means. Someday..." but she was crying hard and he couldn't understand the rest.

The sight of her sobbing, contorted mouth and free-flowing tears cut through him like a knife. Still he made no attempt to console her. Unable to look at her again, Thomas pulled away from her and trudged out of the abbey and up the hill to his car. Maggie stood still and watched him through an eight hundred year old opening, a thousand dissonant emotions stabbing at her heart, making her weak. She tried to clench her fists and couldn't, instead felt her strength slipping away. She called after him, saying the things she desperately wanted to be true.

"I don't believe you, Thomas. This isn't the end and you know it. Whatever you're scared of, it's not me, not us." No response. "You're going to miss me, you know that? I love you, everyday, always. Don't forget this, Thomas. Don't you dare ever forget!"

Through blurring tears, she watched him drive away along the winding road until he disappeared over the hill.

She felt tired, wretchedly tired. Her shoulders slumped. She got into her car slowly, leaning against the steering wheel. *Home*, she thought, *I need to go home.* "Damn you, Thomas deFremond, damn you," she whispered. Then she sat back, covered her face with her hands, and cried.

* * * * * *

Dusk was falling when she returned to Stag Hall. The sun had found a thin opening and poked through the heavy layer of clouds, softening the steely sky as if to soothe her, whispering, *Don't despair, things will be better soon.*

Maggie closed the door gently, hoping no one would hear her enter. At the end of the hall, however, Eamon had been pacing the length of his room anxiously awaiting her return. He opened the door and with one look at her knew what had happened.

"Hullo". She didn't want to look at him because she

knew that if she did she'd fall apart, but then she did anyway, her knees giving out, and she crumbled to the floor. Eamon flew down the hallway and caught her, cradling her in his arms.

"There, there Mags, it'll be alright." He led her to her bedroom and set her down on the side of her bed, rocking her. Between sobs she blurted out her anguish.

"He's scared, Eamon, he's running away. I would've gone with him but he wouldn't let me. He said he wants to forget me, forget everything, as if we didn't exist."

Eamon didn't answer. He said nothing. He had promised. He just rocked her back and forth, rubbing her shoulder, feeling her jerky sobs against his warm chest, murmuring to her that everything would be all right. He closed his eyes, wishing he had the power to make it so.

* * * * * *

At first, Matt didn't recognize Thomas's voice on the other end of the line. He sounded strained, his tone one pitch higher than normal. Plus there was a faint clicking on the line...barely detectable, but he noticed it once, and then again.

"Everything's fine here...yeah, normal. I heard about Pennton, though. They're saying they don't know yet if it was an accident or foul play. You okay?"

"Yeah, I'm okay. Don't react to what I'm going to tell you, especially if Philip's around, okay? Ian Pennton's apartment was blown up, with him in it. No accident."

"Whoa. You know this?"

"Yeah, that's what the investigators told us. Matt, I'm not in Ireland now. You're going to be getting something by

Federal Express. Watch for it, okay? It won't have my name on it. Check to make sure it's sealed. Now, go into my office and shut the door." Matt pushed the hold button, did as instructed, and picked up the phone in Thomas's office.

"I'm back."

"See that Keats poem on the wall next to my desk, right by the lamp?"

"Keats? Yeah, I see a poem here, Thomas, but...".

"Good," he interrupted, "now this is what I'd like you to do..." Matt listened carefully to Thomas, straining to hear his soft-spoken instructions, baffled but trusting.

* * * * * *

TO: goffing@toulouse.com

FROM: EZWriter

SUBJECT: Job completed

George,

    Attached is my last installment. I'm coming home. Need to know, can I start on my next assignment right away?

TO: LazyJane

FROM: EZWriter

SUBJECT: home

Eamon took me to the Hill of Tara, Jane. I asked him to stay below at the car so I could be there alone for awhile. No click of the camera this time. Eamon has caught the beauty of this place on film already. This trip held such private purpose for me, I didn't want a camera or the diversion of an assignment to interfere.

You must come here someday and stand on it like I did. Kings reigned and were buried here, Jane, and you and I descended from them! That was the romantic part of Tara's fascination. Much more than that, its beauty has a mesmerizing allure. I trod upon the dips and rings of earthworks where clans performed their royal rituals for centuries. I waited for the Stone of Destiny to speak to me (but heard nothing conclusive) (smiling), and tiptoed around the Mound of the Hostages.

For company I had only an undisciplined flock of sheep, who ambled along the wooded edges of one rim of the Hill. The velvety rich green grass tempted me to remove my shoes and walk around barefoot, and were it not for the sheep shit all over the place, I would have (that part won't go into my story for George). Up there you could see for miles, and I listened to the silence and watched the clouds roll in and the afternoon turn to dusk before I could tear myself away.

Sitting at the top of Tara was an epiphany for me. I felt as if I were breathing in a healing salve, so I collected as much into my lungs as possible. I have a lot of healing to do yet, Jane, and so do you. It's time for us to have that long talk and shed the past together, yes? Put the coffee on, will you please? And tell Charlie I need a big hug from him...I'm on my way home.

Miss you, need you,
Maggie

chapter 11

HOME

Land of Heart's Desire,
Where beauty has no ebb, decay no flood,
But joy is wisdom, Time an endless song.

William Butler Yeats

He'd thought the traffic in Belfast was unnerving, but Minneapolis was nuts. These Americans drove way too fast for his comfort, especially in this ice and snow. He clung to the armrest in the back seat as the taxi sliced between cars and weaved back and forth across the lanes on Interstate 35 heading for downtown. His relief was obvious when the gruff-looking driver pulled up to the lobby entrance at the Hyatt on Nicollet Avenue. The meter made a final click, and the driver looked halfway over his shoulder to the back seat.

"Sixteen dollars." Eamon handed him a twenty and climbed unsteadily out of the car.

"Keep the change." The driver had already released the trunk and jumped out ahead of him to help unload his luggage and video equipment. Time was of the essence in the taxi business.

A youthful bellman with reddish cheeks and sunny, Scandinavian good looks helped place the cases on a cart and followed Eamon into the lobby. He'd never been in such a big, fancy hotel...certainly there were none like this in Belfast. So this was what Thomas meant when he arranged for Eamon to come to Minneapolis and said, "I'll put you up in a comfortable little place in my mother's style." Thomas had insisted on using his inheritance from Meryl and Thomas Senior to finance the production. "I don't have any better use for it," he'd said, "this way I can guarantee it'll be handled our way."

At registration, the clerk immediately handed Eamon his keys and told him someone had already checked him in. The bellman directed him to the elevators and led him behind the luggage cart onto an empty car. After a brief awkward silence, the boy started to whistle a tune. Eamon didn't recognize the melody. He kept his gaze straight ahead toward the crack in the elevator door and gradually picked up the tune, whistling along with the boy until the elevator stopped and another passenger got on. The door closed, the elevator jiggled and started moving, and Eamon and the boy resumed their tune, their delighted, mischievous eyes never exchanging a glance even when the third passenger turned to look at them curiously. When the car stopped on seventh floor, Eamon stopped whistling, winked at the young man, handed him a tip and said thanks, he could get it the rest of the way from there.

"Are you sure, sir?"

"Aye," Eamon said and tugged the cart through the sliding doors. He didn't want company when he got to his room.

"Have a good day, sir!" As he pushed the cart down

the hall, Eamon heard the boy's soft whistle above the hum of the ice machine and the closing elevator doors.

Sure enough, as he unlocked the door and swung it open, his eyes immediately swept the floor and caught sight of the half-inch thick Federal Express envelope lying a few inches inside the room. He glanced up and down the hall and found it empty. Swiftly he pulled the luggage cart into the room and leaned down to scoop up the envelope. Closing the door and latching the deadbolt, he turned the envelope over and read the address — "Eamon Loftus, Guest, c/o Hyatt Regency, 111 Nicollet, Minneapolis, Minnesota, USA 55425" — and a return address indicating the package had been sent from London.

Eamon ripped open the outer Federal Express package, removed the inside envelope, and felt along the edge of the flap. He inspected the clasp and was pleased to find no signs of tampering. Pulling a pocketknife from his pocket, he slit it open and pulled out a smaller, manila envelope. It was labeled simply, "Yeats". He laid it on the bed, walked over to the window and threw open the drapes to let in the warm sunshine. Then he picked up the phone and dialed.

"Thomas...mission accomplished. You enjoyed the pages of Keats poetry?" He listened a moment, nodding. "Aye, who knows whether the 'Keats' on your package fooled them, but it was a grand relief to find the 'Yeats' envelope waiting for me." He listened again. "I'll call her today and let you know how she is. Aye, see you then." He hung up and started dialing again. Two more phone calls to make.

"Paddy? Aye, it's me. It's here, all's well. Our grand scheme went off without a single hitch. Is the professor there with you? How's he healing? Good, will you tell him? Aye, see you both in a few days. Kathleen and Ceil are in the States already? Brilliant! Goodbye then." He pressed the button to disconnect, stared at the receiver, and let out a deep sigh of relief. *Now then,* he thought, h*ow do I begin to explain all this to Maggie?*

* * * * * *

The temperature was in the forties, unusually mild for a Minnesota winter day, and the sun was shining. Maggie needed to get out for a walk. She yanked on her jacket, closed the door of her house and stepped into the bright morning light, squinting. Tufts of melting snow clung to glistening evergreen branches and dripping icicles tapped out a cheerful surrender to the promise of oncoming spring. The air in Minneapolis felt thinner and drier than the misty softness of eastern Ireland. Still, it was comfortable and familiar.

She walked leisurely down the block, sometimes looking around, sometimes watching the sidewalk in front of her, side-stepping puddles of melting ice that collected in the corners of cement squares. Distracted by the mud that threatened to muck up her hiking boots, she temporarily focused on avoiding wet spots on the sidewalk. *Step on a crack, break your mother's back*, the childhood adage played and replayed in her mind, mingling with the thoughts that continued to emerge from her heavy heart.

The game got tiresome and she lifted her head to look around at old familiar sights — the rows of houses with expansive front yards, family vans and sport utility vehicles, so typical to Americans, parked alongside the curbs. Invariably, as had happened so many times recently, her thoughts drifted to memories of her life as it was a few weeks earlier — Irish villages, tiny cars parked half on the sidewalk and half on the street because the roads were too narrow to pass otherwise, the easy drone of conversation in pubs, the trickling streams and curved paths under low-hanging branches, the cool feel of moss on abbey stone, Thomas's smile and his firm embrace. At once comforted and sad with the images that appeared, she resolved to forgive Thomas and try to move on. The trouble was, she didn't want to move on. She missed him. And she was mad at him — no...angry, she was damned angry.

The phone rang insistently as she opened the door. Wiping her feet, she made large hops across the floor to pick up on the fourth ring.

"Mags! How are you keeping? Eamon calling." He had this funny way of casually talking as if they'd seen each other just the day before, despite his excited anticipation of hearing her voice.

"Eamon! Where are you? Here? At the airport? I wasn't expecting you until tomorrow!"

"Actually, I caught an earlier flight in and thought better of bothering you. I'm already settled in at the hotel."

"No bother, Eamon! Silly bird! How about if I come over right now?"

"Brilliant...can't wait to see you."

* * * * * *

Over dinner, Eamon and Maggie chatted away easily about their jobs, Eamon's new assignment that brought him to the U.S., and the successful completion of their documentary. They carefully avoided what was on both of their minds, though each knew that the subject of Thomas would inevitably come up. Neither wished to risk the joyfulness of their reunion, so they continued to steer their conversation away from the question Maggie wanted to ask yet didn't want to ask and the long, complicated explanation that Eamon wanted to give that he hoped would ease her mind.

For the next few days, they spent as much time together as possible. Maggie brought Eamon to the office to meet George and her colleagues at Toulouse, and then she took time off from work at George's urging to spend with Eamon. When he wasn't taping footage on the assignment that brought him to Minnesota — a video documentary comparing life along the Shannon and the Mississippi Rivers — the two tooled around town, walked the path along the Mississippi, and recaptured the fun of their Irish adventure at Kieran's Irish Pub within hiking distance from Eamon's hotel.

One day shortly after his arrival, Maggie parked in the hotel ramp and rode the elevator up to seventh floor to pick him up for an evening out. Eamon let her in and went back into the bathroom to finish shaving. While she waited, Maggie looked around the room until her appraisal stopped at the desk next to the window. She pounded on the bathroom door, not waiting for him to come out.

"Eamon! You didn't tell me you've finally joined the age of technology! When did you get a computer? This is terrific! Don't tell me you actually know how to turn it on?"

He opened the bathroom door and leaned out, wiping shaving cream from his face with a towel. "Funny," he rejoined, "not only can I turn it on, but I've got an email address... been trying to figure it out, but I'm not much good at the moment."

"Then let me help you, okay? I'll give you my email

address, you give me yours, and we'll say good night tonight via Internet."

Hours later, the cold remains of a pizza sat in a box on the edge of the bed and the two friends huddled over the computer. Eamon had become initiated into the world of Internet chat. They had entered a room called "Irish Pub2" and joined the conversation. To Eamon's surprise, the banter felt almost as if he were sitting on a barstool chatting up and down the length of a bar. When they said goodnight and logged off, Eamon was hooked. Maggie yawned, stretched, and looked around for her purse and keys.

"This was fun, Eamon. I learned a lot about your strategies with the opposite sex. You didn't have much trouble being yourself, ol' RathlinLad," she grinned, referring to his online name.

"Can we do this again soon? There was a certain girl in that room I want to try to find again...I think her name was MaureenO57."

"Sure...tell you what. Let's see if you've got it figured out. When I get home, I'll call you and then we'll both log on and go back into IrishPub2, okay?"

"Grand. Let me walk you down to the car and see you off." At her car, she turned and looked at him.

"Eamon, I'm so glad you're here. The past few days have been...well, very good for me." She reached up on her tiptoes and hugged him, then kissed him softly on the cheek. That moment — perhaps it was the lateness of the hour, or their easy companionship, or the fun of the evening, but it seemed right, and Eamon kissed Maggie back. On the lips. Gently. She kissed him back, then pulled away, wondering what she was doing...what they were doing. She fumbled with her keys and turned around to open the door. After she got in, she looked at him again, not knowing what to say.

"Later." She couldn't think of anything else. So she just smiled.

"Later," he said. He sighed as he watched her drive off.

* * * * * *

All the way back she wondered what led to that kiss that seemed not exactly romantic, not exactly one just between friends. Trying to analyze it, she became more confused and told herself not to analyze, but she couldn't shake the thoughts running rampant through her head. When she got home, her mind was a muddled mess. She attempted to clear it by rearranging the shelves and drawers in her study, throwing out old material and straightening with ruthless precision the papers in each file folder, whose tabs of course were organized in perfect order and without deviation in left, middle, and right third cuts.

Realizing suddenly that Eamon would be waiting, she dialed the hotel.

"Maggie, where've you been?"

"Oh, sorry, Eamon, I got waylaid with stuff."

"Stuff?"

Tired, not wanting to explain, she replied, "Eamon, let's just go online." That was too abrupt. She softened her tone. "Eamon?"

"Yeah?"

"I had fun tonight. I'm glad you're here."

Eamon was silent for a second, then said, "Me too."

"See you in a few minutes online?"

"Okay."

Maggie logged online, signing on as GalwayDrm, a new name she had registered when she returned home from Ireland. She navigated to the chat rooms and entered a virtual room called "IrishPub2." No sign of RathlinLad at first, and she watched the chat, occasionally keying in a comment. After a few seconds, she saw his screen name pop up on the list. She sent him an instant message.

GalwayDrm: Sorry. Ta-daaaa! You made it!

RathlinLad: Aye, a wee dizzy from the ride, but I'm here, all right.

GalwayDrm: Well then, let's see if Maureen's still in here or if you have to cruise around for her.

RathlinLad: Grand.

Below their instant message, the chat room conversation evolved with its continually changing occupancy.

"Howdy from a Yank...are the natives restless?" a new visitor, Cavanbound, had typed.

Along with a flurry of responses, Maggie typed in her own welcome. "Hey there, Cavanbound, care for a spot of tea?"

* * * * * *

Thomas had been trying for several minutes to get online and cursed the inconvenience of his Internet provider's growing pains. This time, however, he logged on easily and found mail waiting for him, signaling with the enthusiastic voice of an announcement: "You've got mail!" Mail already? he wondered and then recalled the usual welcome letter from the service. He headed again for the chat rooms, contemplating which room to try and opting for the familiar "Over Forty" group he had visited occasionally the past year.

He watched the dialogue scroll up his screen, found some old acquaintances chattering away and almost responded to them. Then he remembered, *I've got a new name, they won't know me.* The idea of being a stranger again didn't bother him, he rather liked the anonymity. He exited the room and double-clicked on "Irish Pub2". The scrolling dialogue moved fast, and he typed, *Howdy from a Yank...are the natives restless?*

Responses from several people popped up on the screen. *Welcome, boyo, How's tricks across the ocean? What time is it over there...we're pouring Guinness, would you like a draw, lad?*

As he read the responses, he saw his name appear on the bottom row of dialog; he backed up and read it again. Someone was addressing him. The screen name startled him — GalwayDrm. Thomas sat back and stared at the screen. Again the dialog scrolled up and Thomas joined in.

GalwayDrm: Hey there, Cavanbound, care for a spot of tea?

Cavanbound: Thanks, but I've got some. Now if you want a good cup of tea, allow me.

GalwayDrm: Go for it, honey, I expect you know how to boil water.

Cavanbound: That I do, my dear, learned it from an expert.

Guinnessbygosh: Ah, Laddie, make it a Guinness, if

you know what's good for you. Best to start celebrating St. Patrick's Day a wee early, I say.

Agreement with the suggestion from several roommates popped up on the screen, and Thomas chuckled.

RathlinLad dropped off the list and didn't return. Maggie didn't notice right away, having struck up a conversation with the new visitor. It was only when she turned out the light and was thinking about her conversation with Cavanbound that it occurred to her that she hadn't said goodnight to Eamon.

* * * * * *

Eamon was busy the next week, and Maggie needed to get caught up at work. She was planning a story that would take her to San Antonio to cover the old city's preparations for its annual Fiesta in April. She would cover various aspects of Fiesta — the cultural diversity, the festivities, the music and arts, the history, the weeks of work of various committees to plan parades, the colorful decorations, and the city's inherent reverence in its historical monument, the Alamo. There was much to prepare and George had been unable to locate a photographer yet. She wondered if she could talk Eamon into staying on for a few more weeks and partner with her on this new story. His inexperience with American culture could lend a fresh perspective to the pictures and scenes they would record.

Eamon seemed quiet, preoccupied, but Maggie gathered that he had work on his mind, with his new project in full progress. When she returned home Friday afternoon, she found a message on her answering machine from him.

He asked her to meet him at Kieran's, there was something he needed to talk with her about. She found a booth toward the back of the long, noisy pub and thought about her strategy to persuade him to sign on for the Texas job.

"We're wrapping it up a week from Tuesday," he said when she asked him how his current assignment was coming along. She wondered why he seemed preoccupied.

"Then what?"

"Then I've got another job right away."

She was disappointed but not defeated. "How long will that one take?"

Eamon glanced at her, then down. "I don't know. Why do you ask?"

All strategy was thrown to the wind and Maggie blurted out her idea. "Eamon, I'm going to San Antonio in a few weeks. Come with me, work on that job with me. It'll be fun for you and me and great for us to work together again."

Eamon slumped back in the booth and fidgeted with his glass, not wanting to meet her eye. "Maggie, there's something I need to tell you." He took a long, slow sip of his ale and signaled to the barmaid for another. Just beyond the barmaid he saw someone and quickly looked back at Maggie.

She saw the change in his expression. She searched in the direction he'd been looking. Puzzled, trying to figure out what he had seen, suddenly she stopped and stared. There, at a low table on the other side of the bar, sat Kathleen and Ian. She reeled with the shock of recognition. Ian! He's alive! And though his back was to her, she couldn't fail to recognize the other man. Sitting there with Kathleen and Ian was Thomas.

* * * * * *

During the explosion at Pennton's apartment, Eamon explained to her, the professor had been injured but not killed. He had suffered some nasty burns and cuts that required stitches, and his right arm and a couple of ribs had been broken when he was thrown against the kitchen cupboards by the blast, but otherwise he was all right.

Immediately after the explosion, Ian had called Paddy, who secreted him away before the authorities showed up. Paddy had quickly deduced that someone wanted the device badly enough and would do anything to get it. He left Ian in the care of a friend who could be trusted not to talk, a doctor who treated his wounds. Then Paddy went on to meet Thomas and Maggie back at the bombsite. When Eamon joined them, out of earshot from Maggie, the three men used the explosion to contrive a deception.

Kathleen and Ceil had been brought into the secret, and they even enlisted help from Father Carroll, who had reluctantly agreed to conduct a bogus funeral. But they had all agreed that Maggie would be safest if she were kept in the dark along with everyone else...no more people should be involved than necessary.

"Eamon, you could have trusted me. I could have helped. How could you leave me out of it? It was horrible of you to let me think he'd died!"

"Maggie, at the time there just wasn't any other choice. I'm sorry, darlin', really I am."

She shook her head, trying to absorb it all.

Eamon continued to explain: Back in Belturbet while Maggie had grieved and her friends put up a convincingly mournful front, the four men gathered in the sacristy of Stag Hall Parrish and in hushed tones laid out their strategy to smuggle the device to America. Ian agreed that he would have to go there to complete his work, and Thomas could help obtain the patent and arrange financial backing. Then they'd be able to consummate a partnership with Cavan Crystal and ensure it would be manufactured in Ireland.

Thus, almost everything Maggie experienced after the explosion had been a charade, manufactured by her friends to protect her and to fool the industrial heavies who were after the professor's device. Maggie was shocked...she had been completely duped.

Thomas had returned to Manhattan, Eamon told Maggie, and within a few days resigned from Holmes. They had all known he would be watched and his communications monitored — phone, emails, snail mail, everything — so he had canceled all his accounts and started with new ones.

In a plan to divert attention, before boarding the plane for the U.S. he had express-shipped to his assistant Matt a thick envelope labeled "Keats" after English poet John Keats, intending it to appear to be a code. Whoever intercepted it would surely believe the contents contained the plans for Dr. Pennton's invention. Very likely they couldn't know immediately that the material within was altered details for an unworkable piece of equipment.

Their foresight had paid off, because it had indeed been intercepted, its worthless contents copied, and the envelope resealed and forwarded on to Matt. Thomas suspected that the interception had occurred right in the mailroom of Holmes.

At the same time, Thomas had, in his penchant for droll twists and clues, labeled the envelope of authentic plans with the name of Irish poet William Butler Yeats and sent it to the Hyatt Regency Hotel in Minneapolis.

He had also sent a copy of the bombsite videotape by

air express to Matt's home, whereupon Matt used his resourcefulness and Internet savvy to obtain an identification of the redheaded stranger who had been following them. Matt learned that he was a Derry man named Brian O'Neill and that he had been convicted of blasting open a bank vault in Newtownards in 1993. O'Neill had been paroled six months ago. His older brother had been a known IRA soldier in the early nineties, which probably explained how the younger O'Neill developed his skills with ordnance, explosives being his specialty.

The most interesting piece of information about him, however, was that he had been back and forth between Dublin and London several times since his parole, hand-delivering packages for a small software development firm owned by none other than Malcolm Holmes and John Walker jointly. O'Neill had been arrested for the bombing of Dr. Pennton's Dublin apartment, and an investigation into the likelihood of the software company's involvement, particularly what part Walker might have been played, was underway.

Thomas and Eamon had arranged the Shannon-Mississippi Rivers assignment as a ruse to allow Eamon to come to the U.S. His real intention was to join Thomas and the Penntons. Eamon had contacted his friend Jack Manahan, who had emigrated to the States two years before and opened a pub in the heart of downtown Minneapolis. Jack offered them use of a second, unused storage room behind Kieran's, where with a team of technicians, Thomas, Eamon, and Ian completed the flat screen. Now the trio were in the process of setting up a production facility at Cavan Crystal back in Ireland.

* * * * * *

The tightness in her throat as she listened restricted her speech, her emotions playing havoc with her reasoning. Common sense insisted that Thomas had done the right thing, removing her from the danger of the situation; and had she known that's what he was doing, of course she would have resisted and attempted to stay with him. He didn't have much choice but to break ties with her. But the nagging question played on her insecurity about Thomas's feelings for her: How much of what he did was out of love for her, and how much was cowardly reaction or maybe worse, fear of commitment?

It didn't matter anymore, she told herself. The days since their abrupt parting had passed without a word from him. She looked over to the table where they sat and stared at him, his back to her. She had thought they hadn't seen her yet, but now she sensed they knew she was sitting there looking at them. And it was clear that Thomas was ashamed to face her; he didn't turn around even after Maggie saw Kathleen glance at Eamon and then lean closely to Thomas and murmur something.

"Eamon, I don't know how to handle this. What do you expect me to do, just say 'Okay, fine' and laugh about it? I thought the man was dead! I thought Thomas was a coward. Hell, I still think he is!"

She glared at the table on the far end, and as she did, Thomas slowly turned around and faced her. She watched in a daze as he stood up, excused himself from the others, and started to cross the bar toward her. She panicked, afraid to talk to him. She jumped up and darted from the bar, shaking off Eamon's hand as he tried to stop her, denying to herself that she heard Thomas calling her name.

* * * * * *

Maggie ignored the flashing light on her answering machine and, breathless from her escape, closed the door to her little house and headed straight for her bedroom. Weak and shaky, she dropped onto the bed and wept. She cried in anger that she had been left out of the scheme to help the professor, she cried in relief that he was alive, she cried tears of desire and loss and shame at having been fooled. Mostly, though, she cried in frustration, not knowing whether she could learn to love unconditionally.

After a good twenty-minute cry, Maggie blew her nose and then propped her head in her hand, leaning on her elbow. *Analyze this, organize it, figure it out,* she told herself. *What do you want? What do you expect?*

Through her tears, she began to think sensibly. This was good, because practicality was her strength, the trait that empowered her to cope with and triumph over every problem she had encountered in her life. It didn't matter whether the problem was minor or monumental, logic was her tool to reach resolution, and instinctively she used it to harness her emotions and determine what to do next. This pragmatism, she knew, came from watching her mother cope through all the problems she had faced.

She admitted to herself that she was a perfectionist as well as being compulsive. Somehow, all the elements that came together to shape her personality — the ordeals of her childhood, expectations of family and friends, conditions around her, and the genes that formed the unique, complex person that she was — had produced a perfectionist. No point in apologizing for it. But to recognize it and learn to temper it when you need to — that was her challenge.

Thomas wasn't by any means perfect. She hiccupped the last of her sobs away and smiled ruefully, picturing his wonderful smile. She started making lists in her head, pros and cons of Thomas. He's funny and smart and romantic. He's messy and annoying. He's persistent. After deciding he possessed more pros than cons, she turned then to the events that Eamon had recounted for her. She had thought Thomas was a coward the day after the funeral at the ruins when he was claiming to run away. Could she still say that after what she knew now? He had hung in with Eamon and Dr. Pennton to get the device finished. He must have done what he did because he believed in Dr. Pennton, was committed to helping him, and because he loved her, not because he was afraid. But he should have trusted her! He should have told her the truth! Perhaps he didn't really love her, at least not enough to treat her as a partner in thick and thin.

Okay, she mused, continuing her analysis of their relationship, we've established Thomas's not perfect. Neither am I...far from it. I don't expect perfection. And I love him. So the next question is...can I live without him?

chapter 12

FRUIT OF THE ORANGE

"A re you going to ignore his calls forever?" Maggie was at the kitchen sink, helping Jane put the finishing touches to dinner. She thought about it.

"I don't know. Back in Belturbet I told him we'd never part, that I didn't believe he was leaving, now I'm not sure I should let him come back."

"Wish I could help you, honey, but I believe that you'll know in time what's right for you. Just don't wait too long, okay?"

Maggie missed her intimate talks with her sister while she traveled. She depended on their confidences and the moral support they had shared from the time they were young girls. Now Jane had listened quietly and intently while Maggie recounted her experiences roaming across Ireland. She cried with her as Maggie spoke of the great relief she felt from cleansing away the emotional sludge left over by their childhood abuse. Together they resolved to help each other through the final healing left to be done. It helped to talk with Jane about Thomas, because Jane could read Maggie like no one else could. She knew how to help Maggie trust herself.

"You'll be okay, Mags, I know it."

* * * * * *

Back home that night she logged on to check her mail. The "instant message" jingle sounded, and the instant message screen appeared.

Cavanbound: Maggie, it's me, Thomas. Please don't leave...wait and hear me out.

She sat back, staring at his name. Tapping the desktop lightly, thinking, hurt all over again, she hesitated.

Cavanbound: You still there?

GalwayDrm: Yes.

Cavanbound: Will you talk to me?

GalwayDrm: No.

Cavanbound: Will you listen to me?

GalwayDrm: Yes.

Cavanbound: I love you.

Cavanbound: You still there?

GalwayDrm: Yes.

Cavanbound: I had to handle it that way, Maggie, do you understand?

GalwayDrm: Yes.

Cavanbound: I trusted you, but I didn't want to risk you getting hurt.

GalwayDrm: That's funny.

Cavanbound: You know what I mean.

Cavanbound: Maggie? You still there?

GalwayDrm: Yes.

Cavanbound: Will you ever talk to me about this?

GalwayDrm: Maybe.

Cavanbound: Can you say anything else?

GalwayDrm: I kissed Eamon.

Cavanbound: You did?

GalwayDrm: Yes.

Cavanbound: Was it nice?

GalwayDrm: Yes.

Cavanbound: He gave me your new online name, you know. As nice as when you kissed me?

GalwayDrm: No. I have to leave now.

Cavanbound: Maggie, wait. I'm going back to Cavan in a month.

GalwayDrm: Yes, I know.

Cavanbound: I want you to come with me.

GalwayDrm: I can't.

Cavanbound: You can't or you won't?

GalwayDrm: Won't...maybe can't. I have a new assignment.

Cavanbound: Think about afterward then? Join me in Cavan after your assignment is done?

GalwayDrm: I'll think about it.

Cavanbound: You will?

GalwayDrm: Geez. Yes. I'll think about it.

Cavanbound: Okay. I love you Maggie, always. I have something of yours.

GalwayDrm: What is it?

Cavanbound: Your Claddagh ring. Let me bring it over?

Cavanbound: Maggie?

GalwayDrm: Not now.

Cavanbound: Okay, I understand. I'll wait. Goodnight, my love. XOXOXOXOXO.

GalwayDrm: Goodnight, Thomas.

* * * * * *

She made him wait three days. She didn't really want to make him wait; that amount of time just felt right. This was the decision of her life. Although she wasn't keen about leaving a decision hanging, she wanted to give herself time to thoroughly sort everything out.

When she was ready, she wrote him a letter and sent it by email.

TO: Cavanbound

FROM: GalwayDrm

SUBJECT: Answer

Dearest Thomas,
*   Leaving Ireland was followed by a seven-day*
withdrawal process for me in which my mind, in

waking and sleeping, was bombarded with hundreds of memories, dreams, and wishes. What's that Ricky Nelson, song... "Dream"?

You know, because you shared them with me, that the memories are a mixture of good and bad. I've been feeling sorry for myself most of the time. But on Sunday I gave myself a lecture, that one about "being happy for what you've got", and it started to work, so I decided I'll just have to repeat that lecture daily for a little while. It just didn't seem to be sinking in as rapidly as my little self-pep talks usually do. And then you showed up here in Minneapolis.

You should have trusted me, Thomas. I could have handled it. I would have kept the secret...I could have helped you. I'm a big girl and I can take care of myself, you needn't have worried about my safety. However, I appreciate the difficulty of the decision you had to make, and I realize we were all in a delicate, even dangerous situation.

I want to share something with you. You know something about my childhood and how things changed for my brothers and sisters and me when Dad left and the horrid stepfather came into the picture. A few years later, when I was eighteen my father died unexpectedly. I hadn't seen him for two years. He had fortuitously arranged to pay off his debts but left only a few belongings behind...some boxes of clothes and books.

My brother Bobby and I were the only children who wanted something of his for keepsake, and together we rummaged through those boxes. I came up with one thing...a paperback novel.

*"Came a Cavalier" by Frances Parkinson Keyes
became one of my favorite books of all time. I think
you'd like it, Thomas...it's about a Red Cross aide
and a captain who meet in Normandy in WWI, and
their story spans the years beyond WWII.*

*Anyway, what I want to share with you is
something I found in the book. Dad had tucked a
little poem, cut out of a magazine, into the pages of
the book. Suddenly now I understand that this little
poem, this slip of paper is a symbol to me of why,
even though Dad's drinking made our lives
painful, after Mom divorced him I still idealistical-
ly believed he was a great man. Now I realize that
he wasn't great at all, he was sick, but his love for
my mother was inexorable. He and I shared not
only a compulsive nature but a romantic one too. I
guess out of necessity, Mom had to suppress her
own romantic ideals and be the practical one of the
two (and I think I must have gotten that from her).*

*So I suppose that's why he carried this little
poem in the book, and perhaps that's why now I
still carry it preciously with me and why I've made
it my talisman of sorts while I hoped with all my
heart that you'd return to me. Here it is...*

*O that we might, for one brief hour
Forget that we are bound apart,
And lie within each other's arms
Mouth pressed on mouth, and heart on heart.*

*For just one hour from all our life
To sink unchained through passion's deep
And, cast upon the farther shore*

To lie entwined in tender sleep!

I've thought this through a million times, and I realize now that you didn't mean to hurt me, that your intentions were right and good. And I realize that I can't live without you, that I want to be with you now and always. I'm here, waiting, and I love you, too.
Maggie

P.S. Thomas, I remembered that song. I believe it's "Then You Can Tell me Goodbye" by the Casinos. It goes like this: Kiss me each morning for a hundred years...Hold me each evening by your side...Tell me you love me for a million years...Then if it don't work out...Then you can tell me goodbye...Sweeten my coffee with a morning kiss...Soften my dreams with your sigh...After you've loved me for a million years...Then if it don't work out...Then you can tell me goodbye.

She hit the "Send" button and logged off. She padded into the kitchen in her thick cozy stockings, humming the song. She put the teakettle on to boil water, placed a teabag in a mug, then slowly dripped honey into it. Ten minutes later she was curled up in her reading chair sipping chamomile tea when the phone rang, and this time she picked it up.